Griswald then walked back to a central position, out of the line of fire, and spoke to the two. "I will count to three in a measured manner, one . . . two . . . three . . . fire. Exactly like that. At the command 'Fire,' you may turn and fire at once, or take as long as you wish—within reason, a moment or two. Is this understood?"

Both men nodded again.

In a different tone of voice Griswald said, "I must ask you once more, does either of you have anything to say before I begin the count? This proceeding can be halted at once."

Neither man moved. Voss growled something under his breath and Griswald said, "Colonel?"

"Nothing."

"Very well," Griswald said. He took a long breath. "I will begin the count." He paused again. "One . . . two . . . three . . . fire!"

Voss turned quickly, aimed, and fired in a moment.

Also by Arthur Moore
Published by Fawcett Books:

THE KID FROM RINCON
TRAIL OF THE GATLINGS
THE STEEL BOX
DEAD OR ALIVE
MURDER ROAD
ACROSS THE RED RIVER

THE HUNTERS

Arthur Moore

FAWCETT GOLD MEDAL • NEW YORK

A Fawcett Gold Medal Book
Published by Ballantine Books
 Published in the United States by Ballantine Books, a division of Random House, Inc., New York, and simultaneously in Canada by Random House of Canada Limited, Toronto.

Library of Congress Catalog Card Number: 90-90301

ISBN 0-449-14656-1

Manufactured in the United States of America

First Edition: November 1990

Chapter One

Reichenbach

Lothar, reigning prince of the tiny Principality of Reichenbach in Central Europe, sent for Colonel Helmar Voss.

"My son wishes to travel to America," he said when Voss stood before him. "He has an idea he would see the Wild West. . . ." Lothar waved his hand as if to say the idea was insane. "You will go along, Voss, to see that he does not get himself killed by some foolishness. . . ."

"America!" Voss was surprised.

"I am an old man, Helmar. This may be the last request I make of you. Bring him back safe."

"Of course."

"I know I have overlooked much in the last few years, and now there are those who would destroy us. The journey may work out for the best."

"When will we go?"

"That is for you to decide. But do it in secret. I have spoken to Knarig and he agrees."

Voss bowed and left the room, much troubled. The doctors had told him that Lothar might last another year, but it would be a miracle if he lived longer. And Knarig was next in line for the throne.

The men whom Lothar had mentioned, who would destroy the throne, were those who swore to kill Knarig because of his publicly stated intention to regain the province that had split off from Reichenbach a century ago. There were things about which young Knarig could not be reasoned with. The underground group preferred Knarig's sister, Nadya, probably because they thought she would be easier to manipulate.

Colonel Voss had known Knarig all his life. He had been the prince's teacher in military subjects, riding and the use of arms, protocol and dress . . . and a hundred others. He well knew Knarig's shortcomings—and they were many—but he must do as he was ordered.

The Principality of Reichenbach kept a tiny embassy in New York City for reasons of trade. The embassy staff was three in number, headed by Gunthar Zeyen. Zeyen was informed by coded wire that Prince Knarig, Colonel Voss, and a servant would be arriving in New York incognito. They would require lodgings and railroad tickets to Chicago. The prince was bound on a hunting trip. Secrecy was stressed. Zeyen was charged not to reveal the royal presence to anyone. He was ordered to deny any knowledge of Knarig's visit, on pain of dismissal.

By these precautions it was believed the Reichenbach underground group calling itself the Sons of Freedom would be thwarted. If they could not find the prince, they could not harm him. If they thought him still in Europe they would not look for him in America.

However, one of the plan's faults was the prince himself. He was a tall, good-loooking young man with features nearly identical to his father's—when Lothar had been younger. Lothar's profile was on every stamp and coin in the land. Every person in Reichenbach would recognize him instantly.

Helmar Voss was nearing fifty, a stocky, immensely powerful man, straight as a poker. He had a dragoon's mustache and close-cropped gray hair. He and Lothar had been very close as boys.

Voss decided to take along Emil Geller as manservant to Knarig. Emil was an ex-sergeant of infantry, skilled with weapons and reliable in an emergency. He had also learned to be a valet, cook, and man-of-all-trades. And he spoke excellent English. Knarig and Voss had both lived and studied in England and were fluent in that language. Prince Knarig would have to get along with only Emil to look after him. Voss was certain that from Knarig's point of view he would be roughing it.

Voss took Emil into his confidence, explaining what they were about. The hunting trip to America's far west was a ploy to protect the prince from the underground.

"Anything else," Voss said, "is smoke and mirrors."

When the night of departure arrived, Emil drove the unmarked coach to the railroad station at midnight, with Knarig and Voss inside. Knarig, in disguise, moved quickly into a reserved compartment and the train pulled out on schedule.

It had all gone very smoothly.

But it had not been a secret.

Reichenbach Castle was a beehive, a rabbit warren; there were a thousand eyes to see and thousands of ears to hear every whisper. A journey by a member of the royal family could not be kept from everyone.

Karl Jung was a young man of twenty-nine, dark and intense. He was a revolutionary and a leading member of the Sons of Freedom. He was resourceful and competent and had wrangled a minor servant's job, with duties that took him to all parts of the castle. He was always alert for information; one never knew when a careless statement might become important.

So when he heard that Colonel Voss would absent himself from his usual haunts for an indefinite period of time, Karl was very interested. What was afoot? Voss was one of the few people close to the royal family, a man who held a special status at court because of his long friendship with Lothar.

When Karl heard that Emil Geller would be away at the same time, he was curious. He and a few expert henchmen began shadowing the two. Did their actions affect the underground organization? Karl and the others constantly feared a royal plot to destroy it.

When Karl, on a fast horse, followed the coach driven by Emil Geller to the railroad station late at night, he was able to squirm close enough in the shadows of the huge building to recognize Prince Knarig! He was astonished that Knarig was making a secret trip. Emil carried their luggage on a small hand truck—luggage meant they were going a long way!

Without hesitating Karl jumped aboard the train and, at the first opportunity, wired his coconspirators. Knarig and his party went all the way to the seacoast, and Karl watched them go aboard a steamer.

Karl quickly discovered that the ship was bound for New York City. Unfortunately he was out of funds, and had to wait until his friends showed up with money and an order from the Central Committee to follow Knarig and make certain he did not return.

Karl took the next available ship and in New York was met by two members of the Movement, Erich Huber and Franz Wenger.

The Reichenbach Embassy was located in a lower-middle-class neighborhood. It stood alone, an old red-brick building with a vacant lot on one side and a side street on the other.

Karl and his helpers were easily able to keep a round-the-clock watch on the embassy and two days later they saw Colonel Voss emerge, get into a carriage, and drive away.

Prince Knarig must be inside!

Erich Huber obtained sticks of Number One dynamite, and Karl slipped into the embassy building through an unguarded basement window. He cut the fuse for midnight.

It blew up precisely at twelve, shook the ground, and tossed debris high into the night sky. A huge pyre erupted, burning fiercely.

Karl and his friends watched from behind a police line with hundreds of other gawkers.

The morning paper announced that no one had survived.

Chapter Two

PRINCE Knarig, Colonel Voss, and Emil were on the train to Chicago when they bought a newspaper during a lunch stop. The New York embassy of a small European country, Reichenbach, had been bombed and totally destroyed. The police considered it sabotage. The members of the embassy staff were missing and firemen were still sifting through the ashes.

Reading the account, Voss was very disturbed. He felt positive the underground had somehow learned that Knarig was in America and had blown up the building in hopes of eliminating him. That they had been willing to blow up an entire building, with no thought for who else might be killed, was a measure of their determination.

Voss code-wired Prince Lothar at once, relating the incident, requesting permission to return to Reichenbach at once, where a proper guard could be maintained. Lothar refused, ordering Voss to go into the interior posthaste. Lothar would contact the United States government requesting aid.

Lothar, through his ministers protested the inhuman and reckless bombing, mentioning the loss of life, calling it an international incident. The New York papers referred to it as a wee mouse biting at the toe of a giant. Lothar demanded protection for his royal son and was politely told to recall him.

The United States State Department, aware of the troubles in Reichenbach, asked why the embassy had been blown up.

The Reichenbach government was forced to admit that Prince Knarig had been in the building only hours before the explosion. It was further admitted that the feared underground organization was obviously at work and would undoubtedly strike again. Did the United States want the death of a royal visitor on their hands?

The United States did not want any deaths, Reichenbachan or American, to stain the ground with blood—as one young State Department spokesman said to the press. The United States was unwilling to involve itself in European internal affairs and urged again that Knarig be recalled.

The Reichenbach minister replied that the prince was on a peaceful hunting trip and that if he were harmed or killed on American soil the world would see that the United States was indifferent to the rights of others.

The United States replied that the prince was free to request local protection, but that the federal government would not interfere in Reichenbachan politics. Since the prince was traveling incognito the United States would only go so far as to see that he was suitably buried if he were killed, but it would not surround him with cavalry.

Nonetheless, the matter found its way to John Fleming's desk, and his superior said: "We don't want an employee of the government mixed up in this, John. The Tanner Organization ought to handle it—but get someone from the Bluestar unit. We don't want amateurs on it."

"All unofficial, huh?"

"Absolutely. Then we can always deny whatever."

"I understand."

Fleming sent for Laredo and Pete Torres.

They sat in Fleming's office and layers of tobacco smoke almost hid the opposite wall. Fleming was a chain cigar-smoker. There was always one burning in his mouth or in the tray beside him.

Fleming, Director of Security-West, seemed unaware of his visitors' discomfort. He was concentrating on a sheaf of papers as they entered; he nodded to them absently and indicated chairs.

Laredo was a tawny-haired young man whose clothes seemed too tight for him. His white shirt strained across a wide chest and his coat pinched thick shoulders. His sun-browned features were regular, with a square jaw, level eyes, and a mild expression.

Pete Torres was slightly larger, a burly, dark man with hair the color of wet coal. He and Laredo were both graduates of the Tanner Training Center, assigned to the elite Bluestar unit. They had met at the school and been posted first and second in their classes. Most of the candidates had failed for one reason or another and been sent home.

The Tanner Organization, and especially the Bluestar people, worked almost exclusively for the government. They were often able to handle assignments that were politically delicate, very secret, or had elements that the government agencies preferred not to touch even with very long poles.

Pete hunched down in his chair, hoping to find fresher air, without much luck. He too was dressed in store clothes, a suit that barely contained him.

In a few moments Fleming rustled his papers and looked up. "Thanks for coming." He sighed. "We've got something the higher-ups don't want to get involved in—but can't help worrying about. So I've been ordered to push it off onto the Tanner Organization. You've heard this before."

"A few times." Laredo smiled.

"And not the last, I expect." Fleming fussed with the papers and laid them down neatly, putting a heavy ceramic frog atop them. "Let me give you the facts. Our government has been talking to the ministers of the Principality of Reichenbach—which you probably never heard of. It's a little country in Central Europe, and for reasons of trade we want our relations with them to continue as they have in the past."

"What kind of trade?" Pete asked.

"I'm not sure. It has something to do with an exotic plant used in cooking. The thing is mostly grown in Reichenbach. Anyway, it would cause a terrible stink from chefs everywhere if the trade were interrupted. They'd write their congressmen, etcetera, etcetera. . . ." He waved his cigar.

Laredo shrugged. "We're not up on foreign trade, John."

Fleming shook his head, puffing the cigar. "That's got nothing to do with what I'm about to tell you. It so happens that the son of the reigning prince is here in the states. His name is Prince Knarig and at this moment he's on a train, headed for Chicago. From there, we're told, he's going out on the plains to hunt."

His visitors exchanged looks.

Fleming continued. "The problem is—someone's trying to kill Knarig. We would rather it didn't happen."

"There's been an attempt?"

"Yes. The Reichenbach Embassy in New York City was blown up. The bombers evidently thought the prince was inside. He had left the building only a few hours before. Two members of the staff were killed instead."

Laredo asked, "How can you be sure the assassin wasn't after the staff and not the prince?"

"Because they could have killed the staff at any time in the last ten years and didn't. But as soon as the prince shows up—boom! We know there is an underground movement in Reichenbach called the Sons of Freedom. They apparently hate the prince and want him removed permanently."

"So he's traveling in disguise?"

"I'm sure he is."

"So you figure some of these Sons of Freedom are here with bombs."

"Yes."

"And you want us to do what?" Pete asked. "Guard the prince or find the bombers?"

"Well, of course, we'd like you to do both. We especially don't want the prince to die here in the States by an assassin's bullet. The State Department thinks it would look bad to the world." Fleming blew smoke. "It's a sticky situation. The government wants to stay out of it—and yet it can't, really. It's all very muddy."

"You can't surround him with Pinkertons so thick no one can get near him?"

"No, we cannot. Knarig is a bullheaded egoist from what I'm told . . . very difficult to reason with."

Pete asked, "Who's he traveling with?"

"Two people. One is a Colonel Helmar Voss—who ranks high in Reichenbach inner circles—and a manservant, Emil Geller. Voss is described as a tough military man, but very sensible. The prince evidently listens to him, and few others."

Fleming had recent photographs of all three and passed them over. Several were of the prince in glittering uniforms and one in civilian clothes. He was a handsome man, tall with dark hair. Laredo thought his nose was rather thin and pointed. Voss was a stocky, powerful-looking man and Geller, the servant, was thin and nervous-looking.

Fleming had documents—very impressive, with gold seals and fancy engraving—for use as their credentials. They did not exactly state that Laredo Garrett and Pedro Torres were officers of the American government, but they implied it.

"Knarig is used to looking at such trappings," Fleming said. "We think these will satisfy him that you're genuine. I will wire them that you're on the way. All right?" He handed over the documents.

Prince Knarig was indeed eager for the hunt. He had seen pictures of the American bison, called buffalo, and he wanted a trophy head for the wall of his study in Reichenbach. No matter that he'd been told there were few buffalo to be found on the plains now. A really good guide should be able to find one or two.

He engaged a suite, under assumed names, at the Cranston Hotel in Chicago and sent Colonel Voss out to buy equipment and hunting rifles. He had Emil insert an ad in the local newspapers asking for a guide who knew his way around the prairies, and sat down to wait.

Colonel Voss enjoyed himself looking through gun shops. He was impressed by the large-caliber Remington rolling blocks and bought two rifles, ready-made cartridges, lead, molds, and patches and carried them back to the hotel.

He showed the guns to Knarig. "Look here, Cesar." He

handed the prince a rifle. "To load you cock the hammer and roll back the breechblock with your thumb, as far as it will go. This extracts a spent cartridge. You slip in a fresh one, flip up the breechblock and the rifle is ready to fire. All in a second or two."

"Very good," Knarig said, hefting the piece and sighting it.

"I am told a practiced man can get off fifteen or more shots per minute—if need be. That fact will be a big advantage if we meet hostile savages."

"Is that a possibility?"

"Indeed it is."

Knarig's eyes showed interest. "Yes . . . it seems a very good rifle." He set it against a chair "Have Emil clean and oil them."

"Yes, Cesar, certainly."

Knarig went to the sideboard and poured brandy into two glasses. "Is there a chance those creatures will have followed us here, do you think?" He handed Voss one of the glasses.

"I don't know how they could." Voss sipped the liquor appreciatively. "But of course we'll take all precautions."

Knarig nodded, gulped the brandy, and went out, closing the door behind him.

Voss smiled and examined the brandy against the light. Knarig drank only the best. He knew the prince was only annoyed by the fact that he was being followed. Probably the danger never entered his mind. The prince had protested at having to leave the embassy in New York by the alley door. Voss had had to talk fast. The fact that the carriage was there waiting probably had made up Knarig's mind.

Voss sighed. The things he had to do for Lothar . . .

Chapter Three

KARL Jung was disgusted to learn from the newspapers that Prince Knarig had not been in the embassy when it had blown up. Two charred bodies had been found, neither of them Knarig's or Voss's.

Karl had planted the explosive without help. But when the blasted and burned-out embassy became front-page news, Erich Huber disappeared.

"He's gone," Franz reported to Karl Jung. "I don't know where. . . ."

"He gave no indication?"

Franz shrugged lightly. "He was worried about murder. He talked of it many times. He was afraid of being hanged."

"Well, we'll get along without him. What we must do now is find out where Knarig and Voss have gone. I suggest we question all the hack drivers in the area."

"You have pictures of the prince?"

"Yes, and Voss too."

It took most of a day to find the driver who had driven three men and luggage to the railroad station from the vicinity of the embassy. The driver recognized Voss from his picture. He had heard them talk about going to Chicago.

Karl and Franz were on the next train.

With the photographs to show, it did not take long to discover where the three were staying—the Cranston.

They took turns watching the hotel and Karl followed Voss to several gun shops and saw him buy two rifles. After Voss had left, the clerk told Karl that Voss had said he and a companion were going on a hunting trip on the plains.

Karl was unhappy about that. He said to Franz, "It will be very difficult to get close to them on the plains."

"Then we ought to make every effort to see they do not get that far."

"Yes. I agree."

Karl went back to one of the gun shops and talked to a clerk about revolvers.

"The Colts and Remingtons are the best," the clerk said, laying a Colt on the counter. "This is a .45-caliber. It has excellent stopping power."

Karl examined the gun and nodded. It felt very good in his hand. "I'll want two of them, with ammunition."

While Karl was in the gun shop, Franz sat in the hotel lobby watching for the prince or Voss . . . neither of whom knew him by sight. He read several newspapers through and had started on them again when Knarig and Voss came downstairs and went into the dining room.

They lingered over lunch, heads together, discussing something, referring often to a paper on the table between them.

Franz got up and strolled near the table and saw that it was a map.

When Karl appeared in the lobby with a heavy package, Franz said, "They're going somewhere all right. But the plains are a thousand miles wide. . . ."

Karl nodded. "We've got to do it here in the hotel. Maybe we can wait in the hall near their suite."

Five men answered the ad in the newspapers for a guide. The first man to arrive was small and wizened-looking; the prince distrusted him at sight and Voss had to turn him away . . . with misgivings. The man had the look of a plainsman, he thought.

He and the prince questioned the next three at some length, and asked them to wait in another room. The fifth man had been drinking and was quickly dismissed.

The three who had been asked to wait had references, though none could be easily checked. Knarig and Voss talked and finally decided on one man, Charlie Bennett.

Bennett was lean and bearded; he had been on the plains since the age of nine, he told them. If anyone could find buffalo, it was he.

It was what Knarig wanted to hear.

Bennett immediately made out a list of the things that would be needed on the hunt. They could go down across the state to St. Louis and get them there—or go on to Kansas City. "Take your pick."

The prince decided they would leave at once for St. Louis.

Emil packed their bags and went downstairs to settle the hotel bill. "Please have a hack stand by in the morning to drive us to the station."

"I'll attend to it, sir."

Emil did not notice the dark man who stood by the desk as he talked to the clerk. His employer, Emil said, wanted to catch the seven o'clock train to St. Louis. He would also need someone to help carry the bags down from the suite.

"I'll have someone there, sir."

"Thank you."

The dark man smiled and moved away.

In the morning Emil was the first out of the suite. He and a hotel bellman lined up the baggage in the hall, including the two cased rifles. Everything checked, the two began carrying the bags downstairs.

Then Colonel Voss walked into the hall, holding the door for the prince.

Karl, watching at the end of the hall, stepped out and, with the pistol in both hands, began firing. The big Colt boomed in the narrow hall, sounding like a cannon. Instantly Voss pushed Knarig back into the room and nearly fell atop him, slamming the door. Two shots splintered the wood but both men were unharmed.

They stared at each other, sprawled on the carpet. "Sorry, Cesar," Voss said. He got up and helped Knarig to his feet, then pulled a pistol from under his coat.

The prince swore. "We haven't lost them! How did they know we were going out this morning?"

Voss shook his head. Cocking the pistol, he opened the door a crack and peered out. No one was in the hall. Chances were, the man who'd done the shooting was long gone. He would not expect a second chance.

"He was excited," Voss said, "and tried to shoot too fast. Maybe he was unfamiliar with his weapon. . . ." He glanced at the prince. "Stay here. I'll look around."

He investigated both ends of the corridor and returned. Several other roomers looked out fearfully. "Were those shots?"

"No harm done," Voss told them. He and the prince went down to the street, where Emil had a hack waiting.

"Should we call the police?" Knarig asked.

"If we do we'll be detained for hours."

"Did you see the man who was shooting?"

"Not well enough to identify him."

Knarig shrugged and got into the cab. "Then let's not miss the train."

Emil jumped up on the box next to the driver as Voss frowned at the buildings around them. A man with a rifle . . . He sighed and got in beside the prince.

John Fleming's telegram caught up with the train before it reached St. Louis. Colonel Voss received it from the conductor and showed it to Knarig.

"The government is sending two men. They will meet us at the Huntington Hotel."

"Only two men?"

Voss made a face. "We must do with what we must. I think the bombing of the embassy changed their minds."

"The newspapers did not mention my name."

"Yes, but after the bomb blast, Cesar, the Americans could hardly ignore you, traveling incognito or not. If you were harmed it would be an international incident and it could not be kept from the papers. The American government has been forced to do something."

"Who are these two men?"

Voss shook his head. "The telegram does not say. Bodyguards, perhaps. We will have to wait and see."

Knarig fumed. "I do not like it at all. They will probably get in the way."

Voss folded the telegram and slipped it into a pocket. "We can return to New York—or go to another city. Are you determined on this buffalo hunt?"

Knarig was astonished. "Of course! Of a certainty! I cannot let this scum upset my plans. I have not come thousands of miles to be turned aside by villains!"

Voss nodded. Knarig was one of the most stubborn men he had ever known. He had been stubborn and unreasonable as a child. It was partly why he got on so poorly with his father. Lothar had his rages, but the father was a saint beside his son.

The prince took his meals alone in the compartment, but Voss and Charlie Bennett sat together in the dining car and Charlie told stories of the plains. Voss was fascinated by Indians, wondering aloud when they would see some.

"You'll see 'em likely, when we reach St. Louis. I jus' hope we don't see none when we git out on the grass."

"On the grass?"

"On the prairie."

"Ahhh, I see." Voss nodded. "Are the Indians dangerous?"

"As rattlers . . . dependin' on which tribe you meet. Is Mr. Smith a good shot?"

They had agreed to call the prince Mr. Smith in public.

"He's a very good shot," Voss said. "Is it true what we read, that the Indians take scalps?"

Charlie laughed. "Sure they do—and more'n that. A lot more'n that." He winked. "But so do we—if the truth be knowed."

Voss's voice dropped. "You've taken Indian scalps?"

Charlie leaned across the table conspiratorially. "Us whites ain't sposed to do that—but we do. And worse. The thing about Injuns, about some Injuns, mind, is that they torture prisoners to death. That's why they's hated. And the Kiowas is worst at it. The worst of all."

Voss could not tell if the other spoke the truth or not. It

sounded like fact but he had heard that plainsmen were terrible liars and exaggerated everything. But Charlie seemed a good sort, easy to get along with.

When they came to the wide Mississippi the train was run onto a huge barge and the brakes set. The barge was trundled across the river to the city at sundown. There the train was chuffed off and driven into a station where the passengers debarked and sought out their luggage.

Emil hired them two hacks and they drove to the hotel, where rooms had been reserved for them. Hot bathwater was carried up to Knarig's suite, and he luxuriated in a copper tub. Voss went downstairs to the bathhouse with Emil.

The next morning they took a hack to the famous St. Louis waterfront and found the levee a bustling place: men loading and unloading steamboats, chanting their work songs; throngs of passengers and visitors; all the noise and clamor that accompanied the work and play. Prince Knarig was fascinated by the waterfront.

Charlie suggested they travel to Kansas City by steamboat and Knarig agreed with enthusiasm. He was delighted when he went aboard one of the elegant boats and would have taken passage the next day—until Voss reminded him that the two government men were due.

Knarig wanted to see Indians. Charlie pointed them out: swarthy, dark, black-haired men in greasy clothes glowering at those who stared at them. There were very few women, none of them looking anything like the stylized pictures Voss had seen.

"They's dozens of different tribes," Charlie said. "Some don't look nothing alike. They dress different and got different customs. Ever'thing about them is as different as a Irishman from a Swede. And they speak different languages—don't understand each other."

"They look like gypsies," Voss said. "We have them in Europe. They are always traveling and are great thieves."

"Not as good thieves as Injuns," Charlie said. "I tell you, them Crows can steal your horse right out from under the saddle when you's ridin' him."

Chapter Four

THE Huntington was an old and very posh hotel. Laredo and Pete had left their store clothes behind and the clerks eyed them suspiciously when they walked in, dressed in jeans and leather.

Yet they were expected, and after asking for Mr. Smith they were taken to his suite.

Prince Knarig looked exactly like his pictures, minus the gaudy uniforms. He was handsome, though with an almost unhealthy pallor. His manner as he inspected them was condescending, but Colonel Voss made them welcome. Voss looked slightly older than his pictures. He studied their credentials and handed them back, and sent Emil for drinks.

Voss asked, "What have you been told by your superiors?"

"We have been told that you, sir," Laredo nodded toward Knarig, "are traveling incognito, that you are bound on a hunting trip, and that certain people are trying to kill you."

"That rather sums it up," Voss said. "Are you to act as bodyguards?"

Laredo smiled. "We are here to insinuate ourselves between you and these fanatics. We hope to prevent deaths and to capture or otherwise disarm the assassins."

Voss and Knarig exchanged looks. Voss smiled. "That is to be desired—their capture."

"I would prefer them dead," Knarig said in an offhand manner.

Pete asked, "Do you know who these people are?"

Voss shook his head. "Neither His Highness nor I have ever seen them—except perhaps at a distance, or for a second or two. We do not know their names."

"What are your immediate plans?" Laredo asked.

"We have decided only this morning to go by steamboat to Kansas City. Our guide, Mr. Bennett, will get equipment there."

Emil entered and gently set a tray containing a bottle and glasses between them. He faded away. Voss nodded toward the tray. "Please help yourselves. Do you know Charlie Bennett?"

"No," Laredo said, glancing at Pete, who shook his head. "When will we board the steamboat?"

Voss turned his head toward the prince, who said, "Tomorrow."

"Does tomorrow suit you gentlemen?" Voss asked. "If so we will secure the passages. Where are you staying?"

Laredo smiled again. "We assumed we would be staying here."

"I see," Voss said. "I suggest you consult the hotel clerk then." He rose, signifying that the interview was at an end. "Please let me know your room number." He went to the door with them. The prince sat down with his back to them and poured whiskey into a glass. He had probably forgotten them already.

As they walked downstairs Pete said, "Let's wire John Fleming and resign."

Laredo laughed. "He's a cold fish—but then, he's so much better than we are, we should make allowances."

"It makes me wonder if we're on the wrong side."

"That thought crossed my mind too."

The desk clerk had no rooms for them. Every room had been booked, there being a convention in town. He suggested they try the Bramwell House in the next block.

The Bramwell was older and more dingy, actually on a side street; it was also much cheaper. They secured a room with two beds and went out to wire Fleming that they'd arrived, spoken to the prince, and pulled their forelocks.

Fleming replied that it was not their job to educate the prince, but to protect him.

Pete said, "What if he makes it impossible?"

"Then I assume he will get a nice military funeral."

"And we will be blamed."

Laredo sighed deeply. "Yes, I suppose so. But he'll be in the casket, not us."

They returned to the Huntington and were informed that Mr. Smith and his companion were dining. They were not allowed in the dining room, dressed as they were, so Laredo wrote out a note, gave it to the clerk, and he and Pete returned to the Bramwell and had supper.

Emil Geller had secured tickets on the *Majestic*, leaving at noon for Kansas City. They went aboard in the middle of the morning and then had coffee in the main dining room while they waited.

Laredo and Pete were given a stateroom next to Knarig's. They looked carefully at every arriving passenger but saw no one who looked like a fanatic. Probably the prince's enemies looked much like everyone else.

They met Charlie Bennett, who was now dressed in buckskins. He seemed a friendly type, easy to talk to. He had in mind to take the prince to a particular spot, well away from any traveled route, where he was sure they'd find buffalo.

"There are isolated small herds of them here'n there," he said confidently.

The prince was a dude, Charlie said—they might have to wet-nurse him. Voss was another matter. He was probably tough as old boot leather. He would have to be told very little. Charlie had a poor opinion of the prince. "He going to get tired as hell of tent life. . . ."

"He might surprise you."

"No, he won't. He'll want his buffler head and to git out."

"We hope you're right," Pete said.

The trip to Kansas City was uneventful. The boat arrived on schedule and they walked off and across the levee and put up at the Traveler's Rest, a new hotel close to the river.

Charlie Bennett took his list of supplies to a mercantile

house where he was well known, then bought six horses, saddles, and equipment. He had planned to buy a light spring wagon to carry their goods, but to his surprise the prince overruled him. They would use pack mules instead. Voss took Charlie aside and said the prince hated the sight of wagons.

At supper, the last evening before they were to start out, Charlie told them he planned to lead them north and west, up along the Republican River, even into Nebraska Territory. He was positive they would find what they were looking for.

Karl Jung and Franz Wenger followed the prince and his group to the railroad station and boarded the train. They found no opportunity to attack the prince. Knarig took his meals in the compartment and went outside it rarely, and then with the colonel at his elbow. They knew Voss was heavily armed.

Karl told Franz they would have to bide their time. "Patience is a virtue. . . ."

"It might not be difficult to kill Voss," Franz said.

"What would that gain us?"

"Knarig would have to get someone else who might not be as efficient as Voss—or he might turn around and go back to Reichenbach."

"Too many 'maybes.' No, we concentrate on Knarig, not Voss. Not anyone else. With Knarig dead our Movement will be satisfied."

Franz shrugged. "Very well."

The prince and his party registered at the Huntington Hotel in St. Louis and Karl and Franz took turns watching it, hoping for a chance to move in quickly to dispatch the prince. But there were three men around him constantly, Voss and two others, one a servant and the other a lean, bearded man who wore buckskins and who was very watchful.

Then, to Karl's disgust, two other men joined the group. One a tawny-haired young giant, and a Mexican who was even larger.

None of his prayers was being answered.

The entire party of six left the hotel in the middle of the

morning and boarded a steamboat bound upriver. Karl and Franz were barely able to cross the plank before it was pulled in. They traveled to Kansas City, sitting across the room from the prince and his entourage at mealtimes, unable to do anything but growl under their breaths.

Knarig never walked the decks except in the company of three men, one in front, one behind, and one at his side. Anyone who approached the prince was subjected to a close scrutiny by well-armed men.

Karl and Franz kept themselves far away so their faces would not become familiar to the prince's group, and they showed no particular interest in the prince at any time.

They walked off the boat at Kansas City frustrated. It was proving far more difficult than Karl had imagined. Would it be possible to kill all of them?

On boarding the steamboat, Laredo at once asked the ship's officers if a passenger list was kept—and found that a complete list was not. Those passengers who signed and paid for staterooms were listed but not the others. And there were many others. Laredo and Pete looked over the list of stateroom passengers, but none of the names meant anything to them. And certainly an assassin would use an assumed name. . . .

Several dozen men on board looked as if they could be hired killers, but of course looks could be deceiving. One of the most villainous-appearing turned out to be, when Laredo engaged him in conversation, a women's ready-to-wear salesman working out of Chicago.

The prince took brisk walks along the deck twice a day, morning and evening, accompanied by Voss, Emil, and Bennett. Laredo and Pete Torres moved among the passengers, watching for sudden moves or suspicious acts, but if the assassin or his aides were present they made no attempt on the prince.

In Kansas City the entire party put up at the Traveler's Rest Hotel and Charlie Bennett made his purchases.

The hunting party was organized and set out much sooner than Laredo had expected. Voss and Emil were professional soldiers to whom campaigning was second nature; like all young men of his country—Knarig had had years of military training, and Charlie Bennett had been—as he said—practically born on the trail.

They were glad to get out of the city. Emil was put in charge of the mules; the prince and Voss rode together ahead of them, and Charlie Bennett ranged with Laredo and Pete out to the sides, looking for trouble.

But it was not apparent that anyone had noticed their departure from the hotel. "Maybe," Pete said, "we have given the assassins the slip."

"Maybe," Laredo said, "but maybe not. We'll know if we get careless, I expect."

A party of six, they had left a rather plain trail, Laredo mused. If anyone wanted to put in a few hours' work he could probably pick it up by way of the purchases, supplies, horses, and mules. Charlie Bennett had told them with a grin that he'd made it very evident to the merchants that the party was going south, not north. But that simple subterfuge, Laredo thought, would not fool a determined pursuer. There was no way to disguise a half-dozen horsemen and five loaded pack mules. A hundred people had probably seen them leave town and take the trail northwest.

It was a well-traveled road in the beginning and they made good time, camping fifteen miles from the city in a little valley where there was wood and water. Emil put up a fine blue tent for the prince. It was larger than the others and set somewhat apart. Anyone wandering by or glancing at the camp would know instantly that a person of importance slept there.

Laredo mentioned it to Colonel Voss. "It rather stands out, doesn't it? Destroys the incognito, don't you think, Colonel?"

Voss looked unhappy. "There are some things I can do nothing about. His Highness requires certain attentions. This is one of the more harmless."

"Not if a rifleman riddles it."

"That could be a possibility," Voss admitted. "But as I

said, I am powerless to change customs—I am sorry to say. Besides, it is the only other tent we have."

Pete Torres eyed the tent and shook his head. "There have been two attempts on the prince's life that we know about. He knows he's a target . . . and yet he sets himself apart to make it easy for an assassin."

"In the dark the tent will not stand out," Voss said abruptly and left them.

Laredo said to Pete. "You don't understand the royal European mind, amigo. He would rather be shot than admit he's the same as the rest of us."

"Poor man," Pete said sorrowfully. "What a childhood he must have had. What were his toys like—dolls made to look like kings and queens?"

Laredo laughed. "We shouldn't make fun of him."

"I feel sorry for him."

The night passed uneventfully. It was the first night they posted guards, each man taking a two-hour stint, all except the prince.

In the morning Emil brought the prince a washbasin and towels, which he used in the tent. Emil then shaved his master and brought him breakfast, setting up a small folding table.

Charlie Bennett was fascinated with the ritual, never having seen such goings-on.

Colonel Voss also saluted when the prince emerged from the tent. He made a morning report, after which they broke camp and continued on their way.

Chapter Five

KARL Jung and Franz followed the prince's party off the steamboat and tagged along to the hotel. Franz sat by a window with a newspaper while Karl shadowed Charlie Bennett and saw him make various purchases. Then Colonel Voss joined him and they went to the stables to buy horses and mules.

Karl did the same. He bought equipment and supplies, a mule and pack tree. He and Franz were ready to go at a moment's notice. It was child's play to watch for and follow the party as it left the city and took the trail north and west.

That night, when the party camped, Karl and Franz crawled close. Through binoculars, they saw the prince's blue tent being erected.

Franz said, "As soon as Knarig enters the tent we can fire into it."

Karl argued, "The range is too far for accurate shooting, and the light is miserable. With the first shot he'll be out!"

"If we both shoot at the same time . . ."

Karl shook his head. "We were too hasty at the hotel. I don't want to make the same mistake again. If we shoot now and miss, it will show them we've followed them. We'll have the best chance if we take them completely by surprise."

"But we might not miss."

"No. It's too much of a chance."

Franz growled. "Maybe we can get closer."

Karl shook his head again. "I don't want one of us to take

the chance of being captured or shot. No. We'll follow them until a really good opportunity comes along.''

Several times in the next few days Laredo thought he had glimpses of riders far to their rear. These might be pursuers, or they might be ordinary pilgrims making their way from one place to another across country, Laredo thought.

When he called his partner's attention to the distant forms, Pete suggested they go and look.

Telling Voss what they were about, they separated and rode back several miles, but saw no one. Making wide circles they examined the rolling prairie with binocs and returned to the others hours later.

Colonal Voss was nervous and edgy about the elusive figures. ''They may be members of the underground,'' he said to Laredo and Pete. ''It's a certainty they followed us to America.''

''We were told about the Sons of Freedom.''

''It's a high-sounding name,'' Voss said with contempt in his voice. ''They borrowed it from your own revolution. But they are killers. And they are very clever. We must not underestimate them. Do you have a suggestion?''

Laredo said, ''I think they're biding their time, waiting for a chance to strike again. If they attack us here on the open plains they'll have difficulty getting away. Do you think they're willing to sacrifice themselves to harm the prince?''

Voss shrugged. ''I don't know. They did not show any inclination that way in Reichenbach.''

''Then let's go on as we are . . . and keep a good watch.''

They saw game—but no buffalo. Charlie Bennett ranged far and wide on his own, saying he did not want a companion; he was used to being a loner. He investigated likely places, but each time he returned to camp he shook his head wearily.

The days were passing, and each time that Charlie came back the prince was increasingly sarcastic. He began to suggest that perhaps Bennett was unfamiliar with buffalo and that they should show him a picture of one.

Bennett took the remarks with good grace—for a time. Finally he told Colonel Voss that if the prince continued to harass him he would pack up his possibles and depart. Voss explained that the prince was only disappointed and frustrated and meant no reflection on Bennett's abilities.

Bennett said, "It ain't my fault the goddamn buff'ler is scarce. I never hunted 'em to death like some folks."

"He doesn't blame you," Voss assured him. "Let it blow over your head. He'll forget it tomorrow."

Laredo and Pete Torres also made constant circles about the camps, looking for intruders. They came across tracks now and then that led nowhere. As before, they occasionally glimpsed distant figures, but when they headed toward the strangers the riders disappeared.

"They could be owlhoots," Pete said, "steering clear of sheriffs and posses."

"Or they could be no-accounts selling whiskey to Indians."

"Or repeating rifles."

"But they could be the prince's enemies."

Pete nodded gravely. "He must have quite a few."

They had made camp beside a tiny stream in a cottonwood grove about ten miles from the little town of Hendon—according to Charlie Bennett. It was morning and they were preparing to break camp when the prince was kicked by one of the five mules.

Why the mule jumped and kicked out was not apparent, and which mule had done it was not obvious, but the hard hoof struck the prince just below the left knee and sent him sprawling. No one happened to be nearby at the time, but his yelp brought everyone running. The mules were milling about, pulling at the picket line, as if a snake or small animal had startled them.

Emil reached him first. The prince was clutching his knee, rolling back and forth on his back in agony. Emil and Pete held Knarig while Charlie cut away the cloth and pulled off the boot to lay bare the hurt leg. It was already turning purple.

"We got any whiskey?" Charlie asked Emil. "This-here leg is busted."

"Why d'you want whiskey?"

"To let him drink it. That leg hurts like blue blazes and it goin' to get worse."

Emil ran for the bottle.

Voss asked, "How far to a doctor?"

Charlie looked into the distance. "Maybe ninety mile. If he's in when we git there. Them doctors is allus makin' rounds."

Emil brought the bottle and spoke to Knarig. Charlie said, "Let him drink all he wants. We ain't got nothing else for pain."

Laredo said, "Let's take him to town then. We can try to make him comfortable, and send someone after the doctor."

"All right," Charlie nodded. "We got to splint that leg, fix it so it won't move none. Best thing now is to pour cold water on it, keep the swellin' down."

Emil went to the stream for water. Pete took a hatchet and fashioned splints. They cut a blanket into strips and Charlie bound the leg, saying he had done this several times before. The prince was obviously in great pain but he gritted his teeth and suffered the doctoring, though he quickly drank half the bottle and was drunk by the time Laredo and Pete made a travois out of branches. They used all the blankets to provide cushioning, laid the prince on it, and tied him down.

It took a full day to reach the little town, moving slowly so the travois would cause minimal bumping. They took the course of least resistance and arrived at the town after dark.

Hendon proved to be a tiny burg that had grown up around a stage station. It was a pleasant little place in a shallow valley, with willows and oaks in among the shacks and weathered buildings.

Charlie Bennett had gone off to find the doctor long before they reached the town. He would be gone probably a week, he warned them. "More if I can't find no doc."

Prince Knarig was a sodden lump of man by the time they arrived. He was completely out of his head, snoring a bit now and then, the quart bottle of whiskey empty.

There was no hotel in the little town, but the Indiana Saloon had a second floor and three rooms; Voss rented them all, telling the owner they had a sick man who needed some care. They carried the prince up the stairs and deposited him on a brass bed.

Emil fussed over his master, taking clothes off, making the splinted leg as comfortable as possible. When Knarig came out of his whiskey stupor he would be impossible.

Watching Emil, Pete rolled a cigarette. "How long d'you figure before he'll be up and about?"

"A couple of months, I'd guess, before he can walk on it. The bones ought to knit reasonably well. He's lucky they didn't shatter or come through the skin."

Pete scratched a match. "One other thing . . . It makes him a better target."

There was little anyone, except Emil, could do for Knarig. The servant was constantly busy with food, changing bandages and suffering under Knarig's sharp tongue. Colonel Voss spent a few moments with the prince each morning, and always came away tight-lipped.

Laredo and Pete Torres made daily patrols around the town, looking for trouble but finding none. If there were pursuers they were not in evidence.

The Concord stage passed through once a week in each direction, but none of the passengers ever remained in the town.

The hunting trip had come to an abrupt halt.

Karl Jung, a serious-minded young man, felt a great sense of frustration. Time was passing and he had been unable to accomplish his mission. One day soon he would have to report to the Movement and justify his decisions. They might well be very critical of his efforts. And yet, what else could he do? Prince Knarig had five men with him, surrounding him at all times, and two were very watchful, constantly moving and alert, keeping him and Franz at a distance.

A few times at night, taking enormous pains, Karl had slipped close to the camp. But no matter how close, he had learned nothing. He had been very fearful of being detected and captured. That would be the crowning embarrassment! He could imagine the reaction of the Movement!

Then he and Franz had come upon the mystery. When the hunting party had left the camp, the two had examined the campsite and stared at parallel marks in the earth.

Why had they suddenly appeared? "What could make marks like that?" Karl had wondered.

Franz had suggested, "Could they be dragging something behind the mules? But what for? Certainly not to mark the trail for us!"

"It's curious. . . ."

And the deep ruts had continued, making it child's play to follow the hunting party. The marks led to a small town in a pleasant little valley. Karl and Franz circled the town, but the ruts did not appear again; the party had remained in the town.

Karl rode close, dismounted, and slipped into the town long after dark. A sign told him it was called Hendon. There were the usual houses, shacks, and tents, a freight yard and stage depot, two saloons and a few stores. Nothing else but some corrals and windmills. The place might contain, he thought, as many as five hundred souls. It was probably too small to be marked on most maps.

He went close enough to hear music but did not enter either of the saloons. A stranger appearing suddenly would cause comment. They would look him over and talk about him among themselves.

The prince had doubtless tired of roughing it and demanded a bed and bath, so the party would have stopped here.

He returned to Franz and they took stock. It was impossible to remain near the little town; there was nothing to conceal them. They found a convenient gulley with half caves, so a fire could not be seen from a dozen feet away, and made camp. Probably the hunting party, if it went on, would continue north.

Would it continue? They ought to make sure it was in the town. Franz suggested the prince might take the stagecoach.

"It's unlikely. They'd have to sell the horses and mules, wouldn't they?"

"Yeah, that's right. . . . "

"And you know how stubborn Knarig is. He came here to hunt. I think he'll keep at it. They're probably buying supplies."

"And we ought to, also."

Franz said, "Voss doesn't know me. Why don't I go in and look around?"

Karl considered and finally agreed. "Go in as a drifter. Tell them you're passing through. Don't volunteer any information. Use your eyes, but don't ask questions so anyone might get suspicious. Voss is no fool. . . ."

"All right. But what if they ask? Am I a prospector?"

Karl shook his head. "You know nothing about prospecting! You have no tools. No, you're just a drifter, going to the next town. Stay away from people."

Franz sighed. "Very well."

"But listen. . . ."

"Yes . . ."

Franz set out shortly before dusk and arrived in the little town after dark. He got down in front of the livery barn and the owner, a stout, middle-aged man wearing pants over red underwear and no shirt, sold him oats as Franz stared at the five mules in a side corral.

"Huntin' party," the owner said. "They stayin' over a day're two. Youall headin' for the fair?"

"No. What fair?"

"Over to Flat Rock." He pointed. "Over east thataway."

"No, guess not. I'm drifting north."

The owner nodded and went back into the barn.

The general store was closed so Franz sat in the largest saloon and sipped beer, listening to the chatter about him. Nobody mentioned Knarig.

The town had no hotel but there was a sign in the saloon: UPSTAIRS ROOMS FOR RENT. He asked the bartender if he could rent a room for the night.

The other looked at him oddly. "We only got three and they all taken."

"Is there anywhere else in town I could get a room?"

The bartender shrugged, making a face. "Don't think so. This here ain't Kansas City, friend."

"It certainly isn't. . . ." Franz went back to his corner seat, pleased with himself.

He drank several beers, listening to the chatter about him, until a stocky man came to the head of the stairs in the back, paused a moment gazing around the saloon, then started down.

Franz smiled. The man was Colonel Voss! Now he was positive. Prince Knarig was here, in this building.

Voss went at once to a table and joined two other men seated there. Franz stared at a blond young man and a big Mexican. He realized he had seen them through binoculars, at a distance. He sipped the beer. Up close, they looked very capable and dangerous.

Well, he would be able to tell Karl the prince was definitely here, in an upstairs room. He hadn't actually seen him, but then no one could expect a blue blood like Knarig to sit in a saloon with commoners. And most of all, where Voss was, there was his master.

After a short conversation the blond man and the Mexican stood up and headed for the street door. Franz got a good look at them and they looked even more formidable. He lowered his face below his hat brim as the blond man's eyes swept over him. Then the pair was gone, out to the dark street. They were obviously the two who had provided rear-guard protection for the hunting party, the two who had made it so difficult for him and Karl to get close.

Voss sat in the chair with a beer before him, seemingly lost in thought for a few minutes. Then he finished the drink and got up to mount the rear steps again.

Franz slid out to the street. It was very dark; there was no moon, and most of the stars were hidden by straggling, high clouds. He walked toward the livery barn—then halted in the shadows as he heard the sound of footsteps. The two men had apparently gone to the barn and were now returning. Franz pressed himself into a niche and remained motionless.

The two passed him and halted near the saloon doors to survey the interior.

They held a brief conversation and the Mexican hurried away into the dark. After a short walk, the blond man entered the saloon.

Franz frowned. Were they looking for him? They were certainly looking for somebody! He ran down the street to his horse, mounted, and looked back, seeing no one. No sense taking chances—as he was sure Karl would say. He nudged the horse and headed out of town at a walk. He kept looking over his shoulder, ready to spur the mount into a gallop, but the two men did not reappear.

As he passed the last shacks along the road and moved into the wooly dark, Franz breathed a sigh of relief.

But how could they have been after him? They didn't know him!

Chapter Six

LAREDO and Pete were sitting with Colonel Voss for a few minutes in the saloon that same evening, discussing the situation. Now that they'd taken rooms in the town, why bother riding out in the sticks looking for pursuers? They might be victims of an ambush and anyway, it would be like looking for a needle in a field of wheat stubble.

Voss thought about it for a moment and agreed.

Then Laredo rose, saying he wanted to look in on the horses before they called it a day. He and Pete went out and down the shadowy street to the barn.

The stout owner was sitting in the back, smoking a cigar as he read a newspaper in the mealy light of a sputtering candle.

"Your animals is fine," he told them. "But one of the mules needs a shoe. Yawl want me t'take care o'it in the mornin'?"

"Yes," Laredo said, "please do, but no hurry. We'll be here for another few days."

"Hear you got a sick feller."

"Yes, broken leg."

The owner nodded. "Broke mine once. Hurt like billy blue blazes! Still limp a little bit."

Pete asked, "You the blacksmith in town?"

"Well, I guess I am . . . f'what it's worth. I ain't much on anything but shoes, though. It ain't my proper trade." He puffed on the cigar. "My partner was the blacksmith but the Lord took 'im off last year, dammit! I could name you a half dozen He shoulda took instead. If old Willie was still here, I could go over to the fair."

"We heard there was one in Flat Rock."

"That's right. Goin' to start on Saturday, two days from now. I guess half the town is goin'. We ain't had a fair in these parts for five, six year."

"Why don't you just shut up shop and go?"

The older man grinned. "Well, maybe I will. That's a powerful attraction—powerful." He puffed and looked at the cigar. "And that's a funny thing. . . ."

"What is?"

"They was a stranger in here while ago. Said he was just driftin'. Wasn't interested in the fair. You ever hear of a drifter who wouldn't be hell-bent for a fair?"

Pete and Laredo exchanged glances. "What did he look like?"

"Well, he about half as big as you and dark. Had on a brown coat. . . ." He frowned. "That's about all I remember. You want 'im for something?"

"Just curious." They said goodnight and went out to the gloomy street. Pete said, "He could be in the saloon. . . ."

"Maybe there's more than one of them."

"It's possible. Would they try to get at the prince so soon—I mean, they don't know where he is, do they?"

Laredo shrugged. "We don't know what they know."

They paused at the saloon doors and Laredo peered inside. "I don't see any stranger. . . ."

"I'll go around to the back." Pete disappeared into the dark.

Laredo waited several minutes to allow Pete to get to the back door of the saloon, then stepped inside, eyes darting everywhere. There were several men in brownish coats, but he had seen them in the saloon before and they were obviously well known. But when he and Pete had gone out after talking to Voss, he had noticed a man sitting alone at a corner table.

The man was not there now.

Pete came into view at the back of the room. When Laredo looked at him, he shook his head.

They went out to the street again. The stranger had given them the slip. Something must have spooked him.

Colonel Voss was unhappy to hear about the stranger, and none of them got much sleep that night . . . except the prince.

Karl listened grumpily as Franz told him about the scouting trip into town. "I saw Voss and two of the men in the party. . . ."

"But they saw you."

"If I hadn't gone into the saloon, I wouldn't have seen Voss! Besides, they didn't know who I was."

"Well . . . we know they're staying in the town. That's something." Karl fretted because they did not know why the hunting party had decided to loll about in the town, unless the prince was annoyed with camp life.

Franz said, "They're staying in the rooms over the saloon. There's no hotel. But for us to try to get upstairs would probably be suicide."

"Yes, we can depend on Voss to see that the prince is barricaded." It might take a half-dozen determined fighters to get at Knarig.

Karl was vaguely annoyed that Franz had not learned more. He had showed himself in the enemy camp—though Karl had to admit they probably did not know whom they had seen—so he might as well have stayed long enough to learn something they could use. For him to return again would certainly be a mistake.

It was not a good situation they found themselves in. He and Franz were forced by the terrain to camp too far outside of town. It was impossible to keep it under surveillance round the clock.

Why had *he* been picked for this mission!

Stocky Colonel Helmar Voss was equally unhappy. He worried about their situation in the rooms over the saloon because there were two stairways to watch. One was outside the building; it came up to a door that was kept locked, but was too flimsy to be secure. A strong man, he thought, could smash it open in a moment with a heavy booted foot.

They had rented the three available rooms and the prince slept in the center one, he and Emil in another. The third room, overlooking the street, was locked and unused. Laredo and Pete shared a room at the barn at the prince's insistence.

Knarig was uncomfortable most of the time. The pain in the leg was gradually receding, but any twisting movement could be agonizing. Emil deftly changed the bandages and put cold compresses on the leg to keep the swelling down. But the prince was a poor patient.

It was eight days before Charlie Bennett showed up with the doctor, who drove a rattling buckboard. The physician was a heavy man dressed in black, with long, stringy hair and gold-rimmed glasses. He followed Charlie into the saloon and up the back stairs to the prince's room.

His name was William Larson, he said, taking off his hat and nodding to the prince as they were introduced.

He wiped his glasses and looked at the leg, long, thin fingers exploring gently. He questioned Emil and rummaged in his bag.

"This is a tincture of opium, called laudanum. It will help with pain." He gave the medicine to Emil.

There was nothing further he could do about the purplish-black leg, he said. The bones were knitting well.

"Will I limp?" Knarig demanded.

"Probably . . . a little, depending. I might have set the leg better if I had gotten to it quickly. But in order to set it perfectly now, it would have to be broken again."

Larson glanced at the prince as he said it and Knarig shook his head definitely.

"You will not break it again."

"I don't blame you."

"I will limp if I must."

The doctor rose and nodded. Placing his hand on Emil's shoulder, he said, "You have done well. Continue with it."

"Thank you, doctor."

Outside the room, away from the prince's hearing, Emil asked, "How long will it be until he can get out of bed?"

The doctor made a face, pulling down his lips. "Not long. A week or two. Make him a pair of crutches. He will not be able to bear any weight on the foot but he will get around for short hops." He smiled. "The leg will get better with every day that passes."

"And the pain will decrease of itself?"

"Yes, but keep the leg immobile as much as possible."

The doctor was paid by Voss and then set up office in a corner of the saloon. As the news spread of his coming, patients gathered for several hours.

The laudanum made Emil's life much easier. It allowed the prince to sleep at night also. Knarig relaxed—his face began to lose some of the strain and his voice was less shrill. He longed to get out of the damned bed, and Emil promised it would not be long before he was up and about.

Helmar Voss was the one who had sleepless nights. He sent Laredo and Pete out to make endless rounds about the town in daylight, while he slept as best he could. He stood guard each night with Charlie Bennett.

But the colonel's fears did not come to pass. No enemy assaulted the upstairs rooms, and Laredo and Pete did not turn up any suspicious characters in their patrols.

Voss said in a growling voice, "They're out there somewhere. You can depend on it."

"There are a thousand places to hide," Laredo agreed.

Pete said, "The prince is safe enough where he is."

"That's what worries me," Voss shook his head. "We don't know how many they are. If there are enough of them they could overrun the rooms and kill His Highness in the bed. One quick raid could do it."

If there were a half dozen, Laredo reflected. Emil and Voss, even with Charlie Bennett's help could hardly hold off a group of determined men who came in two doors at once. He said, "I doubt if there are a half dozen. . . ."

"We can't be certain."

Pete asked, "Do you have a plan then?"

"Yes," Voss said. "I want to move His Highness to Bonnet."

Bonnet was the next town on the stage line road, about fifty miles away to the west. It was a much larger place than Hendon, according to the bartender in the saloon.

Voss continued: "We can put him, Charlie, and Emil on the stage and the rest of us follow with the mules."

"Why Bonnet?"

"It's a larger town, and I'm sure we can find safer accommodations there. I'm told it's an easy one-day run, and His Highness is able to stand the journey now."

Laredo asked, "When do you want to do this?"

"Immediately. The stage west is due here in two days, according to the schedule. It's seldom more than half-full. We will bundle up His Highness and no one will know who he is."

Laredo nodded. "But you should go with him and Emil."

"Yes, on second thought . . ."

It was a good plan, to send the prince by stagecoach. The chances were very slim that anyone watching from outside the town would see the prince board. Secrecy was the watchword. By this time the pursuers would be used to seeing the stages come and go.

Laredo said, "What if Pete, Charlie, and I take the mules to Bonnet a day before the stage arrives here? If anyone is watching they might follow us and never give the stage a thought."

"Excellent," Voss said. "Do it that way."

Laredo and Pete went out to the street and Pete rolled a brown cigarette deftly. "You figure those hombres can't count?"

"What?"

"If we do it as you told Voss, we'll have five mules with us, but only three men instead of six."

"If we leave here just after midnight it should be too dark for anyone to count us . . . assuming someone is watching at that hour. We'll be well along the road at sunrise. They might not even notice we're gone."

"Your plan is full of 'mights' and 'maybes.' I think the prince ought to be left where he is."

"I tend to agree with you." Laredo chuckled. "But Voss is in charge—and he's a worrier."

* * *

Eli Webb was one of two employees of the Indiana Saloon. He worked mostly as a bartender, and he was on duty when the prince was brought in and carried upstairs. He was told the man had a broken leg, a not uncommon occurrence, and Eli thought no more about it.

But in the long days that followed, Eli met Voss and Emil Geller. Voss was stiff-necked and Emil was friendly and chatty—though he never said anything about his companions. Both spoke English well, though with German-like accents. Accents were common enough, and Eli thought nothing of them. And then one day, in his hearing, Emil called Voss "Colonel."

That was curious. It excited Eli's curiosity. Who the hell were these people anyway? He tried to question Charlie Bennett, who worked with them, but Charlie fended him off, and he learned nothing at all except that they were a hunting party. He tried to approach the young blond giant and the Mexican, who were usually seen together and often jawed with Charlie and Voss. But the blond man fixed him with a steady gaze on being questioned and Eli hurriedly withdrew.

Two of them were foreigners, so maybe the hurt man was also. Eli had read and heard of foreigners who came to America to hunt. There had been articles in the periodicals. To do that, to travel so far just to hunt, it meant they had to be rich. Eli mentioned the group to his friend, Nate Tinkler.

"They rented all three of our rooms upstairs and they got five pack mules down to the livery. And they dress good. They got money on 'em."

"Oh, you got a plan?"

"Stop foolin', Nate. Course I ain't got no plan. That ain't my trade."

"How many of 'em are there?"

"Six, countin' the man with the hurt leg. And I wouldn't care t'tangle with any of 'em."

"You sure they got money?"

"Hell, yeah, they got money. You don't go on huntin' parties when you're broke. They brought in a doc to look at the hurt man, and they pay their bills in cash. On the barrelhead. They ain't hurtin' for money."

Tinkler rubbed a stubbled chin. He was a lean, wiry man who had spent his life in the shade and had once been the guest of the Territory for three years at hard labor. He was always interested in easy pickings. He never said so, but he looked down on people like Eli who worked for a living.

Eli was pale and nervous, half as big as Nate, a sneak rather than a fighter.

Tinkler said, "Tell me more about this-here group. There's five people and one with a busted leg. What they doin', layin' up here till the leg is healed?"

"I guess so. They ain't mentioned their plans to me."

"Don't smart-mouth me. . . ."

Eli pulled back. "Sorry, Nate."

"Are they all together in them three rooms all the time?"

"No. Two are away every day, the blond one and the Mexican. I dunno what the hell they do. But the others are around the saloon most of the time. Of course, the one with the leg stays upstairs."

"Who are they?"

"I dunno. There's one called the Colonel—I heard Emil call him that one day. I think him and Emil is Germans. I dunno the names of the other ones."

"Who handles the money?"

"So far I seen it's been Voss. He's the Colonel. It seems like he's in charge of things."

"Ummm. He's a sickly little gent, is he?"

Eli stared at the other. "Voss? Hell, no! He's hard as nails!"

Tinkler shook his head sadly. "It don't sound like you got a real easy proposition here, Eli. A man could get himself seriously ventilated tryin' to rob this bunch."

Eli's face dropped. "Then you ain't innerested?"

"I didn't say that. But it'll take some more looking at. Maybe there's a angle we ain't thought of yet."

Eli was glum. "Yeah, maybe . . ."

"See if you can learn more about 'em."

Eli grunted and nodded.

Chapter Seven

LONG after dark Laredo, Pete, and Charlie Bennett loaded their goods and equipment on the five mules. An hour after midnight, when the little burg was asleep, all lights out, they started on the road to Bonnet.

They met no one along the way and arrived in the town very late the next afternoon. They left the mules in a livery stable, then unloaded the pack trees and put them into a barn stall where they spent the night.

The following afternoon the regular Concord came clattering into town carrying the prince, Voss, and Emil.

Knarig was tired out; it had been a jolting trip despite the laudanum and he was out of sorts. They carried him into a hotel and up the stairs to the second floor. Voss insisted on a second-floor room.

The hotel was the Harding, named for the owner; it was the largest and best in town. It had fourteen rooms, a bathhouse, barbershop, and connecting restaurant. Compared to the accomodations they had just left, it was palatial. Voss thought it primitive, but he was pleased with the move. He was certain the security would be much improved and, with any luck at all, the pursuers had lost them . . . for the time being.

Emil's first act on arriving in Bonnet was to find a carpenter. The local newspaper recommended several, and he went to call on one and ordered a pair of crutches made. In a short time Knarig would be able to get up and hobble about. Winter was approaching and the inactivity was making the prince restless; he wondered aloud whether he would get his buffalo before the snows came and made plains travel hazardous.

When the prince was safely in his rooms, Laredo and Pete went to the telegraph office and composed a long coded wire to John Fleming, telling him what had transpired to date and where they were.

Fleming's return wire asked for more information on the underground, but they had told him all they knew. What *they* needed was more information from his end—if that were possible. Could he discover how many were after the prince? Anything at all would be helpful.

Fleming promised to do what he could.

Now that they were in a larger room, the security problem was different. They had a long meeting with Colonel Voss to discuss it; he was somewhat more relaxed now that he had no outside stairway to worry him. Voss agreed that patrols in or outside the town would probably be a waste of time and effort. If the pursuers tracked them here, they would doubtless hide out in one of the hundreds of buildings in the sprawling town.

Laredo and Pete took up residence in a room across the hall from the prince's suite. They were ready for anything.

Eli Webb and Nate Tinkler joined half a dozen others on the street and watched as the prince was carried from the saloon to the stage station. Tinkler wandered into the station where he smoked a cigar, sitting in a corner as if waiting for the coach himself. He sat across the room from the man with the leg splints but could not hear the conversation. However, he could see that the man called Voss and the servant were both well armed. The hurt man also wore a revolver. He did not see the buckskin-clad man and the two others, the blond and the Mexican.

When the dusty Concord arrived Tinkler saw the three board it, and in an hour or so watched the stage rattle off to the west. Eli was right, he thought. Those three had money; they acted as if they were used to getting what they wanted, buying it or taking it. And from their actions he was sure the hurt man was the leader.

As he watched the coach depart he made up his mind. He would follow and wait for an opportunity. There was no question but that Voss and maybe the other had money belts filled with cash.

When he returned to the saloon, Eli had been to the livery. "Their horses and mules is gone. They lit out last night."

Nate frowned. "They tell anybody where they was going?"

"No." Eli motioned the barman for beer. "They went to Bonnet, huh?"

Nate shrugged. The hurt man hadn't been able to ride. That's why he and Voss took the stage. Yes, they would probably all meet in Bonnet. He said, "You sure right—they got money."

"Yeah. You notice their clothes? None of 'em dresses poor. You going to Bonnet?"

Nate nodded. "Think I'll go look around. You comin' with me?"

Eli took a long breath. He had anticipated the question and had an answer ready. He shook his head. "I ain't no hand with a gun, Nate. That's where you shine. I'd prolly git m'self shot."

Nate swallowed the beer and nodded again. It was as he'd expected. Eli would just get in the way. He pushed the glass across the bar, said good-bye, and went down to the barn for his horse.

Karl Jung was more unhappy with each day that passed. Nothing was going right. He could not be positive the prince was in Hendon and he and Franz were nearly out of supplies. They had used the last of their coffee two days before and he had scraped the bottom of the sack that morning for tobacco. One of them was going to have to go into town to the general store.

Karl wondered what would happen if they didn't find the prince. How could they explain their failure? Those at home would not understand the perils he and Franz had faced in the American wilderness.

Franz had been in town recently, so Karl decided to go in himself. He had never been face-to-face with Colonel Voss, but it was possible the other had photos of him, taken in Reichenbach when he'd been arrested. It was possible—but not likely. Was there any way Voss would know his name?

He would just stay out of Voss's way. There were certainly drifters and travelers coming through the town all the time. One more should cause no particular notice. Those sitting in tilted-back chairs along the street would discuss any stranger, of course, but Voss was not of that crowd.

Karl led the mule into town late in the afternoon, when nothing was stirring but dust devils. He rode directly to the general store and went inside with a list written on brown paper. The storekeeper was a young man wearing a shirt buttoned to the neck, with no tie. He wore black sleeves on his arms and an apron about his narrow waist.

"You own the store?" Karl asked.

"My pa does." He took the list and frowned at it.

"Any news?"

The other shrugged and pointed. "Got some papers come in on the stage last week. Only three, four weeks old. Got two left, fifty cents each." He went to fill the order and Karl scanned the front page of one of the newspapers. There were strikes in the East. He said to the clerk, "No news here in town?"

The younger man laughed. "News in this burg? Hell, they ain't been no news in this town since I was borned."

Karl watched the young man put the purchases into a gunny sack. He paid the bill and went out to the mule and tied the heavy sack on the tree. Then he mounted the horse and led the mule up the street to the saloon where he dismounted again.

Karl slid inside warily, but Voss was not in the room. A skinny bartender served him a beer, said he had no news, and went back to the end of the bar, talking with several hangers-on.

There was no way Karl could inquire about Knarig's hunting party without curious questions being asked of him. He remained in the saloon another hour, till it was dark out, without seeing Voss or any of the others. He thought that was curious. Surely at this hour there would be comings and goings. . . .

But when he went outside he noticed the steps to the second floor. People could go in and out of the upstairs rooms without going through the saloon at all.

He fiddled with the mule's pack and waited for as long as he dared, but saw no one on the steps. Then, swearing under his breath, he mounted the horse and headed back to their camp.

That night Franz mentioned something else. They had often seen the big Mexican and his blond companion riding several miles from the town, circling it at random as if looking for danger.

Franz said, "We haven't seen them for several days."

Nodding wearily, Karl replied, "I think they've gone, all of them."

"You know something?"

"No. It's a hunch . . . just a feeling. I'm afraid they've slipped away from us. I saw none of them in the town or in the saloon."

"What'll we do?"

"Pack up. We're leaving."

A coded telegram came from John Fleming in Washington. A team of government investigators had turned up a man named Erich Huber, whom they accused of bombing the Reichenbach Embassy.

Laredo and Pete decoded the message in their hotel room. Huber had been in the United States from Reichenbach for about five years; he had fled his own country and was wanted for revolutionary activities there.

The investigators had found papers in his rooms denouncing Prince Knarig, but on being accused of the bombing he had implicated two others; Karl Jung and Franz Wenger.

Jung, he stated, was the ringleader. He was actively seeking the death of the prince. He had planted the explosives in the embassy.

Fleming's wire said that Huber was obviously a weak sister, that he had deserted Jung, and certain of his information must be considered suspect. However, Fleming was positive Huber had named the assassin. Karl Jung was a dedicated member of the Reichenbach underground movement, sworn to do away with Knarig at any cost. He was known to be smart and dangerous.

"Well, we have some names at last," Pete said. "I wish there were pictures of them available."

"Yes, so do I."

Colonel Voss did not recognize either of the names Jung or Wenger. But he went at once to the telegraph office and sent a wire to Reichenbach asking for information about them.

He also wired Prince Lothar, giving him a report, bringing the prince up to date on what had transpired.

There was a doctor in Bonnet, recently returned from a town farther west. Voss sent for him and the man examined the injured leg, pronouncing it very satisfactory. There was nothing anyone could do now, he said, but allow it to heal.

"How long before I can walk on it?" Knarig demanded.

"You, sir, will be the best judge of that. As soon as it can bear your weight."

"How long?"

"Probably a few weeks." The doctor shook his finger at the prince. "Do not hurry it or you will be flat on your back again." He gave Emil more laudanum and left.

Nate Tinkler followed the stage road to Bonnet. He knew Voss by sight, and when he saw him in the Hotel Harding, he knew he was in the right place.

The big blond man and the Mexican were also in the hotel; he saw them together with Voss several times. Eli had said the hurt man was the leader of this group. Were these men all bodyguards?

Tinkler dared not hang around the hotel. He knew that any of the group would remember him after one look. If he showed up twice or three times they would inquire about him. If they discovered he did not live at the hotel, they might take him aside to ask difficult questions. He was sure they would not hesitate.

That fact made it hard for him to keep them under surveillance. But there were chairs and benches along the street, supplied by merchants, where men sunned themselves. Nate took one of these and kept an eye on the hotel entrance as he tried to figure out his next move.

If the leader of the party had a broken leg, would they all wait for it to heal before they took up the chase again? It appeared that way. They were certainly not making preparations to move on. This meant he had a week or two to do whatever he could.

What *was* his next move?

While he was worrying it, everything changed.

Across the street the hotel clerk came out to the walk, tugging on his coat. His attitude said he was through for the day.

On an impulse, Nate got up and followed him as the man went into the nearest bar. Nate joined him, elbow to elbow, pretending great affability saying he would be delighted to buy a fellow citizen a drink. The clerk was equally delighted to accept, and they chatted.

The clerk was young, in his twenties, a nondescript type, poorly dressed—the hotel probably paid very little. He had lank hair and a hangdog appearance. He was not ugly but far from being handsome. He looks very much like a loser, Nate thought. Probably no one has ever bought him a drink before.

His name was Jerry Wicker, and he had troubles. His boss at the hotel was never satisfied with his work. He took out his ire and his annoyances on poor Jerry. Nate sympathized, saying he had once worked as clerk in a hotel. This was, in fact, a lie, but it gave them a mutual bond.

Nate was careful to ask Jerry nothing about the hunting party. That would come later, when he had a hold on the other. He learned that Jerry lived with his mother; the Lord had taken his father years ago. When the clerk finally left Nate shadowed him home and looked in the lighted window to see him kiss his mother. Satisfied that the boy lived there, Nate returned to the saloon.

He was lolling at the bar the next day when Jerry entered and they greeted each other like old pals. Nate bought the beers. They took the drinks to a side table and he offered the clerk a cigar. To his surprise, Jerry was full of a secret—something he had learned that very day, in fact.

The clerk leaned over the table toward Nate and his voice was husky. "You know what we got in the hotel! You ain't gonna guess!"

Nate shrugged and shook his head. "You got a new owner and he raised your salary?"

"Nothin' like that." Jerry glanced around. No one was near them but he lowered his voice anyway. "We got royalty!"

"What?"

"Royalty! We got a real prince! He's from one of them European countries."

"You sure?"

"Of course I'm sure!"

"Well, I'll be damned!" Nate was astonished. "You mean he's here in secret?"

"That's right. It's sposed to be a secret. They d'want nobody to know he's here."

"Did they tell you that?"

"No—but the way they act. I happened to overhear 'em. They call the prince Mr. Smith."

"Which one is he?"

"Oh, you never see 'im. He don't come downstairs at all. Stays in 'is room 'cause he's got a broken leg. I seen him once, when they carried him upstairs."

"A broken leg!" Nate stared at the clerk and suddenly everything Eli had told him began to fall into place. So that was it! A prince traveling under another name. One of the prince's men was a colonel! Of course! He blew out his breath.

Jerry was grinning at him. "Ain't that some news, huh? I bet there never been a real prince in this territory before." He frowned. "You look like you don't believe me."

"Oh hell, I believe you, kid. I believe you. It's just I'm real surprised is all."

"Yeah, I was sure surprised too."

Jesus! A real prince! It changed all his thinking. He sipped beer and listened to Jerry's prattle with half an ear, making grunting sounds now and then. He was glad when the kid got up to go home.

Probably the prince and the colonel had big wads of money with them. He knew from reading newspapers that royalty always traveled first-class—nothing but the best. And Jerry had told him that the prince had the best rooms in the hotel here, and got lots of service.

If he could get his hands on the money they carried it would be a good haul for sure. But there was another way to get more—a lot more!

Kidnap the prince and hold him for ransom!

Chapter Eight

THERE was little for Laredo and Pete to do. Bored, Laredo talked to Voss, who reminded him that the pursuers had once shot at him and Knarig in a hotel corridor. It could happen again. No one could be sure what fanatics would do next.

"The circumstances aren't the same," Laredo said.

Voss squinted his eyes. "What are you getting at?"

"Pete and I would like to go back to Hendon."

"Just to be doing something?"

"Maybe we can turn up information that will be useful in tracking them down."

Voss pursed his lips doubtfully. "You might lead them to us."

"If they don't know Mr. Smith is here in Bonnet . . . and if we suddenly appear in Hendon, how would they connect the two? We could have come from anywhere."

"Very well," Voss said, slightly miffed. "I can't command you. How long do you plan to be away?"

"Only a few days."

"When will you leave?"

"After dark. We'll take a roundabout route and enter Hendon from the east."

"Good."

They waited till most of the town was dark then slipped down to the stable, saddled up, and walked the horses north through the town and onto the prairie, seeing no one. Miles out, they turned eastward, keeping the North Star over their left shoulders.

They took their time and long after dawn, when the rooftops of the little town were coming into view, Laredo and Pete circled toward the stage road and followed it west into the town.

The station was between stages, one not due till the next day. They had a drink with the manager, who had seen them with the prince's party.

There had been some curiosity about the hurt man, he said.

"Someone asking about him?"

The other nodded. "Eli, over at the saloon was sure innerested in him."

"Izzat so?"

The stage manager was a burly ex-driver who had married and settled down. "A' course, Eli is a nosy gossip. Guess that's why he's a bartender."

"Reckon so," Laredo agreed. "Was he the only one who asked?"

"No there was a fellow with him. Think he was more innerested than Eli was."

"Somebody in town here?"

The manager shook his head. "No, I never seen him b'fore. Didn't catch 'is name."

They thanked him and went across the street to talk to Eli.

But he was not on duty. The saloon owner was behind the bar. Eli was due on the job in a couple of hours, he told them.

Pete asked, "Where does he live?"

"You friends of his?"

"Oh yes," Laredo said. "He'll be glad to see us."

The owner nodded and beckoned them out the back door. He pointed to a road that paralleled the main street. "You foller that to the edge of town and you'll see a shack on the left side with a chicken pen attached to it. He lives in the shack. I think it's the last one on the left."

"Thanks."

They went back for the horses and rode around to the

rutted road, a sketchy, ill-marked lane bordered by a dozen weathered shacks and houses and sheds. The last shack had a chicken-wire fence attached to it, with a few scrawny-looking hens clucking and scratching.

The only door of the shack was standing half open as they got down and walked to it. A short, stubble-face man appeared in the doorway. "What you want?"

"Are you Eli?"

"You ain't a deputy?"

"No." Laredo smiled. "We'd like to talk to you a minute or two."

"What about?" Eli frowned from one to the other. He stepped back into the dingy room as Laredo entered. Pete stopped in the doorway, sniffing. The room smelled of sour food, tobacco, and undefinable things. There was an unmade cot, a black-belly stove with a crooked pipe, and against one wall, two rickety chairs and a small table. The solitary window had greased paper stretched across it and gave little light.

The shack and everything in it, Laredo thought, was only waiting for someone to burn it down.

Eli was very apprehensive. "What you want?" he said again, backing to the far wall.

Laredo said pleasantly, "There was a man staying in the rooms over the saloon where you work."

"Yeah, now I know. I seen you there."

"Yes. The man had a broken leg."

"I heard about it."

Laredo continued, "When this man was put on the stagecoach you were very interested. Why was that?"

"I wasn't! Why'd I care about him?" He glanced at Pete, who had drawn a long knife with a shimmering blade. He stroked it on his shirt sleeve, glaring at Eli.

Laredo said, "There was a man with you. Who is he?"

Eli pressed against the wall. "I don't know no such man."

Pete stepped into the room, reaching for Eli. "Lemme talk t'him!" He brandished the blade.

Laredo fended him off. "Not yet, Pete—he's going to talk to us, aren't you, Eli?"

Eli's mouth opened and closed; he swallowed hard.

Pete struggled with Laredo and the knife blade whisked past Eli's nose. Eli gave a little cry and slid down the wall, clutching himself. Laredo managed to push Pete away.

Squatting in front of Eli, Laredo asked softly, "Who is he?"

"I—I—don't—"

Pete growled, "Give 'im to me. It'll only take a second!"

"Who is he?"

Eli was pale. He gave a great sigh. "Nate," he said, swallowing hard, sniffling.

"Nate who?"

"Nate Tinkler."

Laredo pulled the other's head around. "Where is he now?"

"He gone to Bonnet."

"Why did he go to Bonnet?"

Eli stared at the gleaming knife in Pete's hands and cowered away from it. "He—He f-figgered to hold up the f-feller with the leg."

"Who else was with him?"

Eli shook his head quickly. "Nobody."

"Is Nate Tinkler his real name?"

Eli nodded. "Far's I know."

Laredo stood up and went to the door with Pete. He said softly, "Anything else?"

"No." Pete put the knife away as Laredo thanked Eli.

"Keep this to yourself."

They went out to the horses.

Eli sat on the floor, hugging himself. If that blond man hadn't been there the Mexican would have carved him up, sure. His heart was still fluttering as he listened to them ride away.

"Nate Tinkler," Laredo said. "He probably has a record. We can ask John Fleming to find out what he can."

"Yes. Do you suppose Tinkler plans to hold up Voss and Emil by himself?"

"I doubt it."

"So do I. So he'll recruit some hardcases."

Laredo nodded. "And blast the hotel when they least expect it. They'll be out to kill everyone in their way."

They had supper and hit the trail toward Bonnet after dark. There was no way for Eli to get word to Nate Tinkler to warn him, unless he got on a fast horse and hightailed it to Bonnet himself. It was unlikely. There was no telegraph between the two towns—no wire in Hendon at all.

"Anyway," Laredo said, "If Eli told Tinkler, then Nate would know what a big mouth Eli had."

They followed the well-worn stage road, stopping in the small hours of the morning at the way station for water and a bit of food. A guard with a rifle was sitting on the roof. He got down and unlocked the place, saying there had been an Indian scare only a few days past.

They arrived in Bonnet shortly after midday, tired and hungry.

Voss came downstairs in the hotel and then sat with them as they had a late breakfast across the street. They told him what they had learned.

"Another group to deal with!" He was annoyed.

"All this bunch wants is money," Laredo said. "They're not zealots."

Voss sighed deeply. "Maybe I should move His Highness to another hotel. If they can't find him, they can't harm him."

"I doubt if it's necessary. Do you keep the prince informed?"

"Certainly. I hold back nothing from him."

Pete asked, "How does he feel about being a target?"

Voss's answer surprised them. He smiled. "It hardly concerns him."

"What d'you mean?"

"I mean His Highness is above such matters. He does not allow them to affect his thoughts. You must know, he has lived with such things all his life. Threats are everyday fare."

Pete asked, "Did people shoot at him at home in Reichenbach?"

"No . . . but there is a very vocal opposition to the government. However, there has been no assassination of a royal family member in nearly a century, though there have been several attempts.'' He shrugged. ''But unfortunately His Highness has made public political statements that have caused unrest and threats.'' He lifted his hands. ''Those statements are a great part of the reason we are here in your country.''

''Was it the prince's idea to come here?''

''No. His father, Prince Lothar, insisted on it. He thought with the prince absent, the furor would fade away. But I assure you that now he is here, His Highness will get what he came for, a trophy buffalo head. He is a particularly stubborn man—and for all his faults, he is afraid of nothing.''

Laredo smiled, glancing at Pete, who rolled a cigarette and then felt for a match. ''He has faults?''

''I withdraw that,'' Voss said with a straight face. ''Of course he has no faults.''

Pete lit the cigarette and choked on the smoke.

Chapter Nine

KARL Jung was feeling frustrated and annoyed. He had let Knarig get away from him. The prince was not in Hendon. Franz had said he was in the rooms above the saloon, but he was not there. The bartender did not know where he and his group had gone.

"They just up and lit out," Eli told him. "You come to drink or to ask questions?"

So the party must have gone hunting again.

Except that when he asked at the general store, the clerk said the hunting party had not bought supplies there. "Not a dollar's worth."

Karl asked Franz, "How could they go hunting without supplies?"

"They already had them?"

"No, I doubt it." Karl frowned. "It means they did not go hunting."

"But they've taken the mules!" Franz protested. "I saw them in the corral by the barn."

Karl shook his head, growling. "No . . . we've been outfoxed. That damned Voss is clever. Somehow he's arranged this to lose us." He motioned. "Where's that map?"

Franz unfolded it. His finger pointed. "Here's Hendon, where we are now."

Karl studied it. Not many towns. "The two nearest towns are Bonnet and Flat Rock."

"There's a fair in Flat Rock."

"A fair?"
"It's like a carnival. I heard about it in the saloon."
Karl rubbed his chin. "A fair? Do you think they'll go?"
"Yes, if it took the prince's fancy. He's probably never seen one."
Karl nodded. "You're right. If it took his fancy!" He snapped his fingers. "Let's go to the fair!"

Nate Tinkler sent a wire to Ed Vinton. Ed hung out at the Union Saloon in Bolton; they had worked together several times, along with Ed's brother, Will. They were a couple of sticky-fingered gents who had no more scruples than Nate.
He had to word the telegram carefully, but Nate was sure he could depend on Ed to read between the lines. Ed was no fool. He would know that if Nate sent him a wire, it was important and could very well put money in his pocket.
Bolton was only a few days ride away. They should arrive in Bonnet before the week was up.
Nate was right. Ed read the wire, showed it to Will, and they packed their bags, rolled blankets, and set out for Bonnet.

Nate took Jerry Wicker aside. They left the saloon and walked out into a field where no one could overhear.
Nate said, "I need t'know ever'thing you can tell me about this-here prince."
Jerry was startled. "What?"
"You heard me, kid."
"Why you want that?"
The time for buying beers and sweet talk was over. Nate snarled. "Don't be a fool, kid."
"What're you gonna do?"
How dumb could a kid get! "What the hell you think?"
"You're gonna hold him up?"
"He got more'n he needs."
Jerry started to turn away but Nate caught his wrist and held it tightly. "I ain't foolin'. . . ."
"I . . . I d'wanna get mixed up in this!"
"You are in it. All you gotta do is give me information. Who's gonna know?"

"No I ain't in it! Lemme go!"

It was time for the clincher. Nate said, "Lissen, kid, I know where you live. You do like I say and nobody, not you or your ma, gets hurt. You hear me?"

Jerry's head sagged.

Nate prodded. "You hear me?"

The clerk nodded

"All right. You do it proper and none of us goes near your house."

Jerry was surprised. "There's others in it?"

"Of course, five of us . . . and you don't know 'em. One will be watchin' you alla time. Now—what I want is for you t'tell me about all the people around the prince. Things like—what do they do every day? Where do they stay? When is he alone? You understand?"

Jerry nodded helplessly. "I . . . I take food up t'him now'n then."

"Who does it other times?"

"Emil."

"Who's Emil?"

"He's the prince's servant."

"A little skinny feller?"

Jerry's eyes rounded. "Hell, no. He's as big as you. Then there's Voss. . . ."

"I know about him. I seen Emil, too, now I think about it. You tell me where they are at all times. Also the blond one and the big Mexican."

"They got a room across the hall from the prince's."

"All right. When we pull this off, you get a cut. Now go on home and keep your mouth shut. You tell nobody—not your ma, nobody! Hear?"

Jerry nodded. Nate released him and he walked away slowly. His knees felt weak. At the edge of the field he looked back. Nate was watching him.

Jerry sat in his room at home, staring at the opposite wall, seeing nothing. He had been forced into crime. He was now part of a criminal gang! Jerry's heart pounded at the thought of it. He had always been an ineffectual sort; even in school he'd always been a follower, content to do as he was told. He had a starvation-wage job at the hotel; it barely got him and his mother by. What if the law caught him? He'd go to jail and his mother would starve!

But Nate had said he'd get a cut! It would mean a large amount of money! *That* was exciting! He'd be able to buy things he could not afford now. He could even take his mother east—she talked more and more of going there, where she'd been born and raised.

How much was he likely to get? Several hundred dollars anyway. The prince probably had a lot of money in his kick.

The next day at the hotel Jerry kept his eyes open, watching Voss and Emil each time they came near the desk. He jotted down their comings and goings, with the time of each, from the big Seth Thomas clock on the wall.

Voss seldom came down; he usually sent Emil on errands. The servant went out somewhere in the middle of the morning and returned with a package, Jerry noted.

At midday Emil appeared, went to the restaurant, and carried up a covered tray with the prince's lunch. Jerry followed him up the stairs, keeping out of sight, and heard Emil knock on the door in a peculiar manner. Three raps, then one, then three again, and the door opened. Jerry noted that, too.

Later, in the saloon, Jerry related everything he had seen and heard, showing Nate the paper. When he heard about the secret knock, Nate was elated.

"That's exactly what we want!"

He bought Jerry another beer.

Laredo watched the prince take his first tentative steps with the crutches. Emil stood on one side, Voss on the other, not touching him. Knarig could not bear his weight on the foot, but he was able to hobble. He could get from the bed to a chair, and it delighted him.

Emil had found a small footstool, and when Knarig hobbled to the chair he could put the wounded leg up. It still hurt if he bumped it, he said, but it was getting better each day. In a short while they would be able to get back to hunting.

Knarig wanted nothing more than to shake the dust of the hotel from his royal heels.

Laredo and Pete sat in the restaurant with Charlie Bennett that evening. Charlie had been gabbing with wagoners and guides, he said, whenever he got the chance. Several of the plainsmen had told him of seeing small bunches of buffalo, mostly to the north. The buffalo were wary and skittish, though apparently no one but roving Indians was hunting them.

"I told Voss about 'em," the bearded one said. "But he wants to be sure His Honor can ride and get about first, without them damn crutches."

"That will probably be another week or two," Laredo replied.

"Dammit, I hate to sit here doin' nothin'."

"No help for it," Pete said, rolling a brown cigarette. "He won't ride in a wagon like ordinary folks."

"Goddamn picky, you ast me. . . ."

Laredo grinned. "He hasn't our advantages."

After supper Charlie said he had an errand and went off somewhere. Laredo and Pete sat in the lobby reading the latest newspapers that had come in on the morning stage.

Earlier they had received a telegram from John Fleming that turned out to be disappointing. There was no information available about Nate Tinkler. Laredo and Pete would have to get by on what they could discover themselves.

Laredo sat facing the desk, and each time he looked up the young clerk stared at him, then quickly looked away.

Curious. He hadn't paid any attention before but, thinking back, he realized that particular clerk was usually on duty during the day. Why was he here in the evening? Could he be taking someone's shift?

Or was there something sinister in it?

Laredo got up, saying to Pete that he wanted to step outside for a breath of air. Pete nodded absently and Laredo strolled to the door and out to the walk. The street was dark. He hurried across it to stand in the shadows, where he could watch the front door of the hotel but not be seen.

In a few moments the clerk appeared in the doorway, looking up and down the street. He stepped out to the boardwalk, peering around, then finally went back in.

That was damned curious.

When he mentioned it later to Pete, the other thought it odd. "But would a bunch of hardcases have any connection with a young kid like the clerk?"

"He acts like he has."

Pete made a face. "Of course someone could be paying him for information, and he's over-eager."

"Information about the prince?"

"It's got to be about the prince, doesn't it? He's the obvious target for both the political group and Tinkler."

"If we grab the clerk—they'll know."

Pete nodded. "We're just hired hands. We've got to tell Voss and let him decide."

"Yes, I suppose so. But why don't we keep a watch on the clerk and see where he goes, who he talks to?"

"Without telling Voss?"

"Maybe then we'll have something more to tell him."

But that night the watch turned up nothing. If the kid was seeing conspirators of any stripe they were not in evidence. The kid left the hotel and stopped briefly at the saloon, but he talked to no one in particular. Then he went home.

When they told Voss what they had suspected, Voss was edgy and wanted to go at once to the hotel owner to ask him to discharge the clerk.

"On what grounds?" Laredo asked. "We haven't been able to catch him at anything."

"Then why tell me all this?" Voss demanded.

"You're in charge," Pete said. "We tell you everything we know."

Voss said, "That clerk is in a perfect position to detail our actions to someone on the outside. Remember, there was an attempt on His Highness' life in a hotel—"

Pete said, "But if you move the prince to other rooms, the clerk will know it. What will you have gained?"

"Then what do you suggest?"

They stared at each other. Then Pete said, "Feed him false information."

Voss looked back at him, then smiled toothily. "An excellent suggestion! What shall it be?"

Chapter Ten

THE prairie town of Flat Rock was awash in banners and flags. The streets were filled with carts, wagons, buggies, and horses. People had thronged into town from many miles in every direction, starved for entertainment of any kind. The fair provided almost everything that could be desired—or nearly so.

Karl and Franz entered the town on the fourth day of the fair and found the hotel full. Most people were out in the fields around the town and slept in wagons or under them. The entire place buzzed with music and conversation till the late hours.

Because the town was so crowded Karl and Franz separated, to better search out the prince and his party. They first tried the hotels. When Karl described Voss and the prince to the hotel keepers they all shook their heads. "They ain't here, sorry."

They didn't seem to be anywhere.

They rolled up in blankets in the fields like everyone else and searched all the next day, looking at every face, into every likely cranny. They attended every event, were present at every contest and judging.

The prince was not in Flat Rock.

"If he isn't here," Karl said tiredly, "Where is he?"

"He's hunting," Franz said, looking at the rolling prairie. "He could be anywhere out there."

They made a fire, broiled meat for supper, and slept on the grass. The prince had given them the slip.

The weekly newspaper in Bonnet was the *Clarion*, edited and published by Horace Verne, once of Philadelphia. He had come west at the request of his family, lest he embarrass them in society. For a number of years they had paid him to stay away. Horace had a temper.

But in his early thirties he had founded the newspaper, and it had flourished. He was able to use it to take out his spleen, and people enjoyed his brash style and fearless reporting. Now, in his fifties, he was well established and a strong voice in the town council. He was a big man, rounding out in the middle, with a shock of dark hair and a patrician face.

One of the newspaper's most popular columns was titled "In Town and Out." It generally contained folksy items concerning visitors and their doings: "Mary Williams is in town to visit her brother and his family," or, "Mrs. Simon Weeks gave birth last Tuesday, a seven-pound boy. Mother and husband doing well."

It was an innocuous column as a rule. Horace had a boy go round to all the hotels each week to make a list of visitors for the paper, and it was in this manner that he learned of someone registered as Smith who occupied the best suite in the best hotel. A little more digging by a reporter turned up additional facts. Mr. Smith had a manservant and a traveling companion.

This was unusual. Horace knew he was onto something when he read the report. Obviously the man, Smith, was traveling incognito. Who was he? No one named Smith, of course. Possibly someone important.

No matter what, Horace smelled a scoop for his newspaper. He wrote and published a largely made-up story about the enigmatical Mr. Smith, suggesting he might be a highly placed official or perhaps a stage star. He turned the white light of publicity on the enraged Prince Knarig.

Knarig sent Colonel Voss to call on the publisher.

Voss stormed into Verne's office. "You have no right to invade a person's privacy, sir!"

Horace, smoking a long cigar, smiled at his angry visitor.

He was never so happy as when stirring up a hornet's nest. "I have every right. I publish a newspaper. Who is this Mr. Smith, anyway?"

"That is none of your affair."

Horace blew smoke at Voss. "I'll make it my affair."

"If you do, you'll suffer for it!"

Horace looked the other over, head to foot. The man was well dressed, not some country bumpkin. "Tell me something. Why are you here instead of the so-called 'injured party'? Is Mr. Smith afraid to come out in daylight?"

"Mr. Smith is afraid of nothing." Voss pointed his finger. "I warn you, print nothing else about him." He turned on his heel and walked out.

The visit only whetted Horace's appetite for more information. He assigned his best reporter to get into the hotel and ferret out every scrap of information about the man in question. "I don't care how you get it. . . ."

Colonel Voss reported his impression of the publisher to Knarig. "The man is impossible to reason with, Cesar. He is a big fish in a small pond, and he will do as pleases him. I fear there is little we can do about it."

The prince sat in a chair, the crutches on the floor beside him. "That is one of the weaknesses of democracy. A man such as that can poison the minds of all about him with his lies!"

"We have one recourse. . . ."

"What is that?"

Voss shrugged. "In another week you will be able to travel again. We will leave this wretched place behind."

Knarig nodded, sighing. "Yes . . . and not a moment too soon."

Horace Verne's reporter was a skinny young man named James Freeland. Behind his back everyone called him Nosey, for his industriousness. He loved nothing better than to meddle in other's affairs. He went to the hotel at once and interviewed the owner, Mr. Harding.

Harding said, "Mr. Smith is a guest in my hotel and that's all I or you need to know. Don't you go pestering him."

"Of course not," Nosey said. "Have you met this Mr. Smith?"

"No, I haven't."

Nosey then interviewed Jerry Wicker. "Who is Mr. Smith?"

"I got no idea."

"You can find out." Nosey prodded him. "There's ten dollars in it for you."

Ten dollars! Jerry considered. That was three weeks' wages. How would Nate Tinkler find out if he told Nosey? Ten dollars was more than he'd yet received from Nate. All Nate gave him was promises and threats.

"Well," he said, "lemme see the ten."

Nosey put the bill into Jerry's hand and closed his fingers around it. "Its yours. Now who is he?"

"You won't tell nobody I told you?"

"Absolutely not."

Jerry pocketed the money with a sigh. That had been almost too easy. He should have asked for more. "Hold up your hand and swear you won't tell nobody where you heard it. You could get me into trouble and lose my job."

Nosey held up his hand. "Jesus. I swear. I swear."

"All right." Jerry glanced around, but they were alone. "He's a prince."

It was the last thing the reporter expected to hear. "He's a *what*?"

"He's one of them European princes."

Nosey stared at the clerk. "Are you sure?"

"Of course I'm sure."

Nosey took a long breath. "What country is he from?"

Jerry shrugged. "Germany, I think. Voss and Emil both sound like Germans. My cousin once—"

"Who're they—Voss and Emil?"

"Voss pays all the bills and Emil is the prince's manservant."

"I'll be damned." The reporter scratched his chin. "A German prince in Bonnet! What's he here for?"

"They were hunting and the prince broke his leg."
"Broke 'is leg?"
"Yeh. That's why he's here in the hotel. Soon's his leg heals they'll be going."
"What's his name?"
Jerry frowned. "I dunno. I never heard. Emil calls him Highness."
Nosey licked his lips. This was a *story*! Horace would dance around the room! There might even be talk of a bonus.
Jerry said, "You promised!"
"Sure, sure, kid. I remember. All right. Anything else?"
"No . . . I don't think so. But you leave my name outa this."
"I will." Nosey thanked him and hurried down the street. Doc Wanner's office was on a side street. He ran up the steps and rapped on the glass door panel. Mrs. Wanner opened the door. "Yes?"
"I gotta see the doc."
"Are you hurt?" She looked him over.
"No, no, no, I'm a reporter. Where is he?"
She led him down the hall to the office. Wanner was sitting under a green shaded lamp, writing at a desk piled high with papers. He looked up over his glasses. "Oh, it's you, James. What is it now?"
"This's official business, doc—just a quick question or two."
"I see. For the newspaper?"
"Yes, of course." Nosey licked a pencil. "Did you go see or treat a Mr. Smith at the Harding Hotel lately?"
"Yes." Wanner nodded and shrugged. "The man has a broken leg. Is that news? Your paper must have fallen on sad days."
"It's news because of who he is. I don't think his name is Smith at all."
The doctor took off his glasses and wiped them. "All right, Mr. Freeland, reporter. But I don't give a damn what his name is. I will tell you I treated him for a busted leg, and that's all. Please run along. I'm busy." He put the glasses back on and turned to his desk.

Nosey got up and went to the door. "Thanks." He went out to the hall, paused, and came back. "How soon can he travel, would you say?"

"In a buggy? Tomorrow. On a horse . . . ?"

"Yes, on a horse."

"A week or two."

"Thanks again." Nosey hurried out and down the street, feeling excited. A real prince!

He ran up the steps to Horace Verne's office in the newspaper building, grinning like a gargoyle.

Horace glared at him. "What're you smirking about?"

"You won't believe what I got!"

"What won't I believe?"

"Who Mr. Smith is."

Horace sat back and laid his glasses on the desk before him. "You want me to guess, for crissakes? All right. He's the Prime Minister of Tennessee."

"No. He's a prince."

"A what?"

"I told you. He's a prince from one of them European countries, Germany."

"Holy Jesus!" Horace leaned forward. "Are you sure? You checked this?"

"I paid the hotel clerk ten dollars to find out . . . and he ought to know. He sees them every day, talks to 'em. The prince has a manservant and someone named Voss to handle details."

"A manservant!"

"Yeah. You know anybody got a manservant?"

"I'm damned. What's the prince's name?"

"The clerk doesn't know. He's heard Emil, the manservant, call him Highness."

Horace reached in a drawer for a cigar and smiled, showing strong, square teeth. "Jesus! A real German prince here in Bonnet!" He struck a match. "We'll give it first-class treatment. I wish to hell we had a picture of him."

"He stays in his rooms. He's got a broken leg. That's why he's here in town."

"A broken leg—has Doc Wanner seen him?"

Nosey nodded. "I just talked to the doc."

"Then Wanner knows what the prince looks like. Send an artist to see him." Horace lit the cigar and puffed heartily. "You go see what else you can dig up. This'll be the story of the year!"

Chapter Eleven

COLONEL Voss received a return wire from Reichenbach saying that little was known about the man Karl Jung. He had been arrested several times for revolutionary activities and had served a sentence. The foreign minister could provide no other details.

Voss fumed. The information wasn't nearly enough to do them any good. The description provided would fit thousands of men.

But suddenly Karl Jung was pushed out of his mind by a new threat—Horace Verne and his damned newspaper. Verne was determined to plaster news of the prince all over his sheet and there was absolutely nothing they could do about it.

Voss wired Washington, D.C., the State Department, protesting the intrusion and exploitation in the strongest terms. He was told the federal authorities could do nothing to stop an editor from printing the news.

Voss raved. "What kind of a country is this?"

He was told it was a free country, but the information did not set well with him. Voss shouted that a country that allowed people to do as they pleased could not last! It would crumble of its own weight. . . .

Prince Knarig interrupted the tirade. He was restless and tired of this town. "Pack our things. We will leave here at once."

* * *

Nate Tinkler rented a shack on the edge of town and when Ed and Will Vinton showed up they met there, sitting around a table with glasses and a bottle under a smoky lamp, as Nate told them what he had run across.

"He's a real live prince from Europe. Got all the money in the world."

"I never seen a prince," Will said. "Do they look like us?"

"They got better clothes," Nate told him. "This one got a servant and four others around him that come and go. He's at the Harding Hotel on the second floor. I even know the secret knock to get into his room."

"Five agin our three. . . ." Ed pointed out.

"They come and go," Nate said.

"So what you figger?" Ed asked. He was as big as Nate, but shorter. Both the Vinton brothers were short and stocky, dark as alley cats and unshaven. They were built like stumps, some said.

"We go up to the room, give the knock and get in," Nate said. "We take him down to a wagon at the back and drive to the old Ferguson place. You know where that is?"

Ed nodded. Ferguson had died last year and the house was standing vacant. It was a perfect place to hold somebody, being off by itself. "Who are them five around him?"

"A man named Voss. He's like a foreman. Then the servant, Emil, who is with the prince most of the time. Then there's a blond man and a big Mexican—bodyguards, but they stay across the hall when they are in the hotel. There's another one, a guide, but he ain't around much. I only seen him once, so they's really only four."

Will asked, "You sure the prince got money?"

"Of course he got money. Them kind go first-class."

Ed said, "All right, we hold the prince at the Ferguson place. Who's goin' to pay the ransom?"

"The government."

"This here gover'ment? Why would they do that?"

"Because," Nate said patiently, "they don't want no prince dyin' on their hands, do they? The Germans would raise hell. Beside, the German gover'ment will pay back the money."

Ed said, "It means Pinkertons."

"You scared of some Pinkertons?"

"No. But what I hear, the goddamn gover'ment is slow as hell about payin' their bills."

Nate was annoyed. "Lissen, this'll be one of them international incidents, like you read about in the papers. Germany is goin' to scream at the federals and they will pay off quick so's the prince don't get hurt." Nate thumped the table. "Them politicians, they protect each other."

Will grinned. "We c'n send 'em one of the prince's fingers . . . or an ear. That oughta wake 'em up."

Ed nodded. "Good idea. How much you figger to ast for?"

"What about a hunnerd thousand?"

"Jesus!" Will said. "That much?"

"They'll pay it," Nate assured him. "They think a lot of them princes in Europe."

Ed took a long breath. "All right. When d'we do it?"

"In a day're two. . . . Pretty soon."

"Not in the daytime?"

"No. Hell, no. We do it at night." Nate grinned at them. "But first things first. We got to steal a wagon."

Colonel Voss was in a snit. He was upset and feeling grumpy because of Horace Verne's threats to publicize the prince. Not only would the underground movement be helped by it, but every crook and outlaw in the countryside might well come into town hoping to dig money out of the royal visitor.

He made quick plans. Laredo and Pete would hire a carriage at once and bring it around behind the hotel at midnight. They would spirit the prince away in a camouflage of secrecy.

With the subject gone, maybe the newspaper would lose interest.

Laredo and Pete had been keeping a close watch on the clerk, Jerry Wicker, but so far they had learned nothing. The clerk *had* acted suspiciously, but perhaps they were wrong to suspect him.

"Give it up," Voss said when Laredo told him. "Get the carriage and we'll forget this town."

The livery had a light buggy for rent but it was small, a two-passenger affair that could not be closed in. There were also two buckboards and a cart. No carriage. The liveryman said, "Nobody in town needs a carriage."

"Do you know if anyone in town owns one?"

The liveryman nodded. "Oh yes. Miz Linnet had one. She died 'bout six months ago. I guess it's still in her barn. Her daughter lives in the house now."

They went to see the daughter, who had forgotten about the carriage. She was a stout woman with graying hair. She walked to the barn with them and stood with hands on her hips as Laredo pulled the carriage into the yard. It was covered with dust but generally sound. It was an unhandsome rockaway, built for two, with a driver's seat in front and a carryall behind. The glass windows had been removed and replaced by canvas curtains. Underneath the dirt it was a dark green with red trim.

The daughter was delighted that someone wanted to buy it. "I got no use for the thing."

They carried buckets from the well and gave it a quick washing, applied grease to the axles and moving parts, and got a horse from the livery to pull it.

By evening it was ready.

Voss and Knarig had consulted and decided to go to the next town north, Wendover. It was about the size of Bonnet but nearly a hundred miles distant. Neither the stage nor the telegraph went there direct.

Laredo had told Voss that he and Pete suspected the hotel clerk was giving someone information about the prince. And Pete had suggested they feed him false items. What could it hurt? When Voss paid the bill, the clerk would know that they were leaving. So near the hotel desk, with the clerk listening, Voss told Laredo they would leave town by the stagecoach.

* * *

That day, within hours, the local *Clarion* came out. It was delivered all along the main street. On the front page was the story about a German prince in their midst, complete with a drawing, said to be his likeness.

It caused a sensation! People gathered in the street and in the hotel lobby, asking to see the royal visitor. No one of them had ever seen royalty before.

The Town Council sent a message to the hotel inviting the prince to attend a meeting and address them. A half-dozen people brought letters—mostly requests for money—to the hotel desk addressed to the prince. One letter was written by a man claiming to be a first cousin of the King of Prussia. He wished to present himself in his robes, and have tea with the prince.

The hotel owner and his staff finally shooed the mob out of the lobby but they milled about in the street, drinking and calling for the prince to come out. By nightfall many were drunk and had probably forgotten why they were there, but they still shouted and sang, and several built bonfires in front of the hotel.

Jerry Wicker, when he went off duty, pushed through the crowd and entered the saloon, where he met Nate Tinkler. He had news.

Nate bought him a beer. "What is it?"

"The prince is leaving the hotel. They going away."

"Where?"

"I dunno. But they taking the stage."

Nate was surprised. "The stage?"

"Yeah. I overheard Voss say it."

"When?"

"He said soon. That's all I heard. But the prince is on crutches. He can't hide that."

Nate nodded, satisfied. That was right as rain. He lit a cigar, thinking about it. Them taking the stage was good. He and the Vinton boys could follow it and stop it easy, with rifle fire. The stage would be halted when they downed a horse or two. Then a simple threat to shoot through the thin walls of the coach, and the prince would have to come out.

They would then put him on a horse, leave the others behind, and go at once to the agreed-upon hideaway.

Nate puffed smoke and smiled.

Pete stayed behind at the hotel when Laredo slipped out near midnight to bring the rockaway. It was a dark night. Pete walked the length of the alley behind the hotel, and back. Charlie Bennett sat his horse at the south end of the alley in case trouble came that way. They would leave to the north.

Pete saw no one. The crowd in the street in front of the hotel had thinned to a very few; no one came round to the back.

Laredo returned quickly with the carriage. Emil was watching and immediately Voss came out with the prince, who crawled in with his crutches. Emil packed their baggage in the back boot as Voss got in beside Knarig. Emil climbed to the driver's seat and they were off. It only took a minute.

Pete and Charlie led the way and Laredo brought up the rear. Voss's horse was tied to the tail of the rockaway.

Charlie had scouted the route earlier and led them by back streets to the north road. They met no one at that hour and were far along the road by daylight. Laredo was slightly surprised that it had gone so smoothly.

Halting an hour after dawn, they made a small fire and boiled coffee. Knarig stamped about on the crutches, saying he felt cramped in the little carriage. Voss said he would ride from then on to give Knarig more room.

Charlie said it felt like they were going to a funeral.

Voss stared at him. "We're leaving the funeral behind."

"I sure hope so," Charlie said. "They ain't much to my liking."

The road petered out to nothing in places. Now and then it became a one-track trail, little more than a small animals' route to water. It was not made for wheeled traffic, and the rockaway rattled and bounced as if the wheels would fall off. The prince suffered the miserable ride tightlipped but never once complained. It would have been beneath his dignity to do so.

He was pale and drawn-looking when they halted near dusk. Emil fussed over him, making him comfortable on the ground.

Laredo and Pete rode as rear guards, but no one pursued them, as far as they could tell, and they reached Wendover the next afternoon. There they took rooms in the largest of the two hotels. Voss registered the prince as Mr. Summers.

Wendover was on a flat plain and was about the same size as Bonnet, though more scattered in every direction. It was on a stage line, but the nearest telegraph wire was most of a day's ride to the east, according to the hotel clerk.

The stage line connected with another from Bonnet, many miles eastward, and when the stage finally arrived two days later it brought a stack of newspapers, the weekly Bonnet *Clarion*.

Laredo bought a copy and read it with Pete on the walk in front of the hotel. The lead item, in heavy black type, proclaimed: EUROPEAN PRINCE IN BONNET!

Horace Verne had outdone himself. The article was soggy with sarcasm, thick with ridicule—and outright slander. It spoke of the prince as an arrogant, uppity German, too good to mix with mere commoners. But on being unmasked by a *Clarion* reporter, the prince had slunk out of town with his tail between his legs.

There was a picture, a woodcut, labeled "The Prince." It did not look like him in the least. It showed him with his nose in the air, as if he smelled something awful.

Pete said in a hushed voice, "When Voss sees that he'll explode!"

"The paper is all over town. There's no way we can keep it from him."

When they went into the hotel Voss already had a copy, and Pete was right. Voss screamed when he read the article. His face turned purple and he wadded up the newspaper and flung it from him.

Emil took a copy to Knarig, who gnashed his teeth in private.

Such miserable words were an insult to every subject of Reichenbach, Voss shouted. It was an insult to be wiped out in blood! The editor who had written the scandalous lies must die!

"We will return to Bonnet at once," the prince announced, "and I will face this creature."

"*I* will face him!" Voss cried.

"It is I who have been insulted," Knarig said.

"You cannot defend yourself properly with a hurt leg, Cesar. I will take your place."

"Wait another day, sirs," Emil begged. "Let His Highness rest after the journey. What can one day hurt?"

Reluctantly Knarig agreed.

Chapter Twelve

WHEN they were alone Laredo said, "It's foolish for him to return there. Newspaper editors in the wilds write that sort of thing every day."

Pete smiled. "Not in Reichenbach."

"No, I'm sure not."

The same security measures were in effect in Wendover as in Bonnet. It was getting on toward midnight and Laredo was dressing to make a tour of the hotel when Emil came to the door, rapping softly.

Pete opened it and the servant came in quickly. "I cannot find Colonel Voss!"

"Where have you looked?"

"Everywhere!" Emil was nearly wringing his hands. "And his horse is gone from the stable!"

"He's not on an errand?"

"I asked His Highness. No, he is not."

Laredo looked at Pete, who said, "He's gone to Bonnet."

"Sure as a gun."

"That's what I fear," Emil said. "His Highness is in no condition to defend his honor—not on crutches."

"Get us some food," Laredo said to Emil. "Meet us in the stable in ten minutes."

Emil nodded and ran out.

They rolled blankets, pushed into coats, and found Charlie Bennett. "We're heading back to Bonnet. You stay with the prince, all right?"

"Back to Bonnet! What for?"

"Emil will explain." They hurried down to the stable. Voss had perhaps two hours start. They might not catch up. Emil had food wrapped in waxed paper in two small sacks. They tied them on behind the cantles with the blanket rolls and headed out of town.

Voss was an excellent horseman and well mounted. He knew he would be followed and so did not halt but traveled as the cavalry did, alternately walking, loping, galloping, then walking again.

They did not catch sight of him, but his trail led straight into Bonnet.

They reached the town in the forenoon. Laredo said, "First the newspaper office."

The offices and pressrooms were housed in a gray stone building on a side street. The place was quiet. An older man with a green eyeshade met them at a counter when they walked in.

"Mr. Verne isn't in," he told them. "He's gone to visit a sick relative."

"Where is this relative?"

"Sorry." The man shook his head. "He didn't say."

Pete asked, "Has anyone else asked for him this morning . . . maybe someone with a slight accent?"

"Yes, there was a man in here a while ago. I told him just what I told you."

"When do you expect him back?"

"Mr. Verne is unpredictable. I couldn't say."

"We know the man who was here before," Laredo said. "He wants to do Mr. Verne harm. We're here to stop it if we can."

The older man nodded, looking at them more keenly. "Horace—I mean Mr. Verne, always goes armed. He's been threatened more times than you can count. Don't worry too much about him."

"Has he someone with him now?"

"I don't know."

They thanked the man and went out to the horses. Laredo said, "What would you do next if you were Voss?"

Pete chuckled. "Find a place to sleep. He must be tired to death."

"Yes, and so are we. Let's ask at the hotels for him."

The clerks they talked to shook their heads. No one of Voss's description had taken a room. The clerk at the Harding was not Jerry Wicker. "Jerry quit the other day," he told them. "Don't know where he went."

The colonel's horse was not in the livery stable. The stableman said, "He prob'ly taken a room somewheres. They's a hunnderd rooms f'rent in this town."

They found that to be all too true.

It took an entire day to locate him.

He was not surprised to see them. They talked in his room, and he was determined to even the score with Horace Verne. The prince and all Reichenbach had been terribly insulted, and since His Highness could not properly defend himself at this moment he, Helmar Voss, would do it for him.

"What do you mean?" Laredo asked. "Are you going to walk into his office and shoot him? You're not a murderer."

Voss growled. "There's nothing else to do! He must pay for this!"

"But that's not the way."

"Fight a duel," Pete said.

Voss bristled. "He's not a gentleman! A duel is out of the question."

"A duel!" Laredo glanced at Pete. "A brilliant suggestion."

"I am a college graduate," Pete said.

"That's the answer," Laredo said to Voss. "That's the way it will go. Then the law won't be after you."

"I don't care about the law!"

"You will if they put you in a federal prison. All right. We will be your seconds. We'll call on Verne and arrange the details."

Voss growled and protested, but even he could see that it was the best way. And after all, he would get his shot at Verne.

Dueling was against the law, but the local law seldom

intervened in such matters when duels occurred. Each man had an equal chance, or so it was believed.

Horace Verne came to his office the next day. Laredo and Pete called on him, and to Verne's astonishment, explained that they were acting for Colonel Voss, who demanded satisfaction from him.

Horace was mystified. "What d'you mean, satisfaction?"

"On the field of honor," Laredo said.

Horace stood up, his eyes round. "You mean a duel, for crissakes?"

"Yes."

"Jesus! Nobody fights duels anymore! There never has been a duel in this territory!"

"This will be the first then."

Horace stared at them, his mouth half-open. "This is about that story I wrote concerning the prince, isn't it?"

"Yes. Will you write and print an apology in the next edition?"

"Certainly not! I said what I think. The prince is not in his own country now. We say what we please here."

"Yes, but you printed things that are not true. He did not leave with his tail between his legs."

"Are you saying I'm a liar?"

Laredo shrugged. "Even you know you are."

Horace reached into a drawer and his hand closed around a revolver. Then he looked up into the muzzle of Pete's pistol. Horace frowned and relaxed and closed the drawer.

Laredo said, "He could never live it down if he did nothing about such an insult."

"It takes two to fight a duel. I don't agree."

"Then he will come here and kill you."

Horace grunted. "Several have tried."

"Perhaps, but they were not Colonel Voss. I urge you to accept the duel. You will have a much better chance that way."

Horace stared at them.

"He will never give up," Laredo said. "He will kill you

one way or another. You will spend your days looking over your shoulder. And one day he will be there."

Horace sighed deeply.

"Who will act for you, Mr. Verne?"

Horace looked tired. "Bobby Griswald will do. I'll tell him to get in touch with you."

Bobby Griswald was a thickset man, going bald, one of the newspaper's typesetters. He met with Laredo and Pete in the Palace Saloon and they worked out the details. Horace had chosen pistols, as the right of the challenged. It was the only weapon he was handy with.

Each man would fire one shot and one shot only. And upon that firing, satisfaction would be assumed. They would fire from fifteen paces. Dr. Wanner would attend the proceedings.

Griswald said, "I suggest we meet at the east end of First Street. There's a level meadow there, quite a way from any houses. What time would be convenient for your man?"

Laredo said, "These affairs usually take place at dawn, or so I've read. I can't imagine why. Is it a tradition?"

"I don't know. But dawn's too early. Let's make it nine o'clock."

"Fine." Laredo agreed. "Is tomorrow too soon?"

Griswald nodded. "Tomorrow it is." He rose. "I'll see that Doc Wanner is there." He gathered up his papers and went out.

When they told him, Colonel Voss was pleased. "The sooner the better. We're to fire one shot only?"

"Isn't one enough?" Laredo asked.

"I'd like to empty the pistol at him!"

Laredo smiled. "Well, we'll only give you one bullet. Do you have a favorite pistol?"

"Yes." He had a Remington that he was used to. "This will do."

They took the pistol and left him alone. He had letters to write, he said. He did not say, "In case . . ."

* * *

Laredo had entertained notions of tampering with the pistol loads and had discussed the idea with Pete, who thought it a much too shifty deception.

"It probably won't work," he said. "We will all handle the two bullets. Griswald is not stupid. He and whoever else he brings along will not be that easy to fool. And if Voss ever found out about it . . ." Pete rolled his eyes.

"But we don't want Voss killed."

"There's nothing we can do about it now. Let well enough alone. The duel is better than Voss going into the newspaper office with a pistol in each hand. God knows what would happen then."

Laredo sighed. "I suppose so."

"Believe me. I am—"

"I know. You're a college graduate."

In the morning Voss looked fit and rested. If he was worried he did not show it. He had dressed in black, the traditional garb for duelists—let nothing white show for an opponent to aim at. They rode to the field at the end of First Street to find Griswald and another man, Dr. Wanner, and Horace Verne, just arrived by buckboard.

Horace wore a dark blue store suit and looked pale and drawn. But when Laredo asked him formally if he would publish an apology and halt the duel, he refused.

"The man is stubborn," Pete said softly.

Griswald, with Laredo beside him, measured fifteen paces in the brown stubbled field and the two principals took their places unarmed. A number of spectators, attracted by the odd proceedings, had gathered a hundred yards or so from them, whispering among themselves.

Pete had to go and shoo them to a different location, or they would be in the line of fire.

Griswald then stood between the two principals. "You will face away from each other. At the command to fire, each will turn and fire without moving from his position. Is that clear?"

Both men nodded.

Laredo, Pete, Griswald, and the other man, named Courtney, examined the two pistols and the loads, passing them from one to the other till all were satisfied. Horace had brought a big Smith & Wesson; Voss had a .44-caliber Remington.

Laredo and Griswald then went to each principal and handed him a pistol and one cartridge. Laredo watched Voss push the cartridge into a cylinder, then turn it so that when he cocked the piece the bullet would move into place aligned with the barrel.

He said, "Are you all right, Colonel?"

"I'm fine. Fine."

Griswald then walked back to a central position, out of the line of fire, and spoke to the two. "I will count to three in a measured manner: one . . . two . . . three . . . fire. Exactly like that. At the command 'Fire,' you may turn and fire at once, or take as long as you wish—within reason, a moment or two. Is this understood?"

Both men nodded again.

In a different tone of voice Griswald said, "I must ask you once more, does either of you have anything to say before I begin the count? This proceeding can be halted at once."

Neither man moved. Voss growled something under his breath and Griswald said, "Colonel?"

"Nothing."

"Very well," Griswald said. He took a long breath. "I will begin the count." He paused again. "One . . . two . . . three . . . fire!"

Voss turned quickly, aimed, and fired in a moment.

Horace looked as if he had been shoved by a mighty, invisible hand. He whirled about, fired into the ground, and dropped the pistol as he went to one knee and grabbed at his shoulder.

Voss stood glaring and Dr. Wanner ran to Horace with his black bag and laid the other on his back. He removed Horace's coat, revealing a shirt splotched with blood.

Laredo went to Voss, who handed him the pistol. Voss said, "We should have had two cartridges."

"You'd have killed him then."

"The fool deserved it!"

Pete stood by as Dr. Wanner cut away the shirt and dressed the wound deftly. Horace had been hit in the large muscle of the upper arm. The bullet had scraped the bone, Wanner said.

"It'll hurt like blue blazes, but the arm will heal eventually and be like new again," he assured Horace. "You were lucky."

Horace's friends lifted him into the buckboard and Wanner gave one of them a vial of laudanum.

"Give him this for pain. I'll see him again tomorrow."

Voss watched the wagon depart and shook his head sadly. "I fired too fast."

"Spilt milk," Laredo told him. "It's over now. Let's get back to Wendover."

"It's not the ending I had in mind," Voss said grumpily. "He hasn't apologized."

Laredo motioned. "There were enough people watching. It'll be all over town in no time at all. They know what the argument was about. I doubt very much if anyone sides with Horace."

Chapter Thirteen

THE *Clarion* came to Flat Rock by the regular stage, and a bundle of the papers was dropped off in front of the main hotel and quickly put on display. Karl Jung bought one and his eye was caught by a heading in bold, black type.

The prince was, or had been, in Bonnet very recently.

The article that followed castigated him. But it did not say where he had gone.

Karl showed the paper to Franz. "We must go to Bonnet at once."

Franz was outraged. "This article is insulting! Whatever he is, and he is many things—Prince Knarig is not a coward!"

"It is insulting to every subject of Reichenbach!"

"The editor is a fool!"

Karl sighed deeply. "He is an idiot. He even calls the prince a German. But . . . he may know where Knarig has gone."

Nate Tinkler also read the *Clarion* and was disgusted to learn the prince had left town, and not by the stage which he had been watching. Jerry Wicker's information had been bad. Probably Voss had tricked the stupid kid. Nate doubted it would be difficult to do so.

He went at once to the newspaper office, asking for information. Did they know where the prince had gone? The clerk at the counter did not know and the editor, Mr. Verne, was not available. Perhaps the hotel clerk . . . ?

Neither of the Vinton brothers could read. Nate had once seen Will pretending to read a book, but he had been holding it upside down. He did not tell them for several days what had happened, not until they had begun to growl and fret.

When Nate returned to the newspaper office, determined to see the editor—the place was in an uproar. He managed to get one of the employees aside. "What's happened?"

"That goddamn Horace just fought a duel!"

"Who's Horace?"

"The editor. He got shot."

"Who'd he fight with?"

"I'm not sure. Somebody said it was that German prince he wrote about."

Nate shook the man. "Where's the prince now?"

"How do I know?" The man freed himself and hurried away.

If Horace Verne had been shot, there was only one doctor in Bonnet. Nate hurried to Wanner's office, arriving shortly after the doctor returned. He pushed his way in. "Was it the prince that the editor fought with?"

"I don't think so," Wanner said. "I think it was the one called Voss."

"Voss! Was he hurt?"

"No. He shot Horace in the shoulder and they called it off."

"Who was with Voss?"

"Two others. A big Mexican and one named Laredo."

"Not the prince?"

"No. He wasn't there at all."

Nate grunted. "Do you know where they went, Voss and them?"

"No idea." Wanner shrugged.

"Is Horace bad hurt?"

"Yes and no. But it won't kill him, if that's what you mean."

Nate nodded and left.

But he had little trouble tracking Voss and the others out of town. A dozen people had seen them take the road north.

Ed Vinton said, "They prob'ly going to Wendover."

"Then we'll follow and let them lead us to the prince."

It was Pete who first noticed they were being tailed. "Somebody's staying behind, not trying to catch up."

"Let's lose them," Voss said at once.

With Laredo in the lead and Pete bringing up the rear, they left the trail at right angles, following a wide arroyo that headed roughly west and ran almost straight for a mile before petering out. Laredo turned north again, into what appeared to be an old buffalo track.

When they entered a section of jumbled hills, Laredo halted and they examined the back trail, seeing nothing that moved.

Through the brown hills Laredo turned west again, across several miles of undulating high plain that was studded with spiky brush. Then all at once the land became furrowed with straggly trees and deep gullies, difficult to cross. When they came upon a sandy-bottomed ravine Laredo slid the horse down into it, and they went along it at a good pace. They knew they were leaving plain tracks, but as he looked at the sky Laredo knew it would be dark soon.

And when dusk came, they halted.

We can be reasonably sure, Laredo thought, we're miles ahead of any pursuer. Pete dug a deep hole and made a tiny fire, and they ate what food they had.

In the morning they were up at dawn and on the way again. But as they climbed out of the ravine miles later, they were fired at. A bullet creased Voss's hat, slicing an inch out of the brim, but no one was hurt.

In the ravine again, Laredo examined his Winchester. "Did anyone see any of them?"

"I saw two muzzle flashes," Pete said.

Voss remarked that he'd heard four shots.

"Let's set up an ambush."

They found a good spot a mile farther on, tied the horses, and waited with rifles—but no one appeared. They waited an hour then mounted again and pointed north, with Voss grumbling about running from whoever was following them. He wanted to go back and confront them.

But the weather intervened. It turned cold, and in a short while it began to rain. It was a steady, light rain and they continued, heads bowed to the storm.

They neither saw nor heard anything further from the pursuers—Laredo began to wonder it they'd stumbled over some wandering owlhoots who had been trigger-itchy.

They rode into Wendover at night, where the hotel had rooms for them. The prince was fine, Charlie Bennett reported. Nothing untoward had happened since they had gone. He, the prince, and Emil were astonished that Voss had fought a duel. The prince insisted on hearing every detail.

Knarig was disappointed that the editor was still alive, but Voss explained how the duel had been fought. There had been only one bullet for each man, a decision arrived at by the seconds.

The prince was also annoyed to hear they had been fired on and pursued. It was undoubtedly the Movement, he said. He was hobbling about on the crutches with more facility, able to put nearly all his weight on the foot.

He felt well enough to get back to hunting.

Laredo and Pete encoded a message and sent it by the stage line to the next town with a telegraph. They informed John Fleming where they were and of the events up to that point. Fleming was certain to be unhappy about the duel and the publicity it would cause. But they explained it was probably the lesser of two evils. Colonel Voss would have gone into the newspaper office with blazing guns, and might well have ended up in the Territorial Prison if they had not managed to sidetrack him. It was not always possible to regulate other people—especially foreign dignitaries.

Charlie Bennett was given money to purchase supplies, and that done he had them packed on the mules with Emil's help. Charlie suggested to the prince that they go north and west, and Knarig agreed.

Laredo and Pete set out in that direction an hour before

the others, to scout the trail. Charlie marked their maps. They would all meet in two days at a place called the Notches, a collection of rocks and sandstone cliffs.

"Look sharp for Injuns there," Charlie said. "It's on a old north-south track. They been usin' it for centuries."

Charlie was hopeful they would find buffalo near there in one of many small, twisting canyons in the vicinity.

It was raining lightly when Laredo and Pete left Wendover late at night, taking precautions against being followed. They rode all night and in the early morning the rain let up. The day dawned bright and clear, with a brisk wind blowing from the north. They circled far to the east, using binoculars to investigate the distances, but saw no one.

They were at the Notches in two days. In the shadow of the limestone cliffs were the remains of hundreds of old camps, but none recent. At midday they watched the mules plod toward them with Charlie Bennett in the lead.

They had seen no one, they told him, but they'd seen no buffalo either.

Karl Jung and Franz arrived in Bonnet and listened to the gossip in the saloons. There had been a duel fought between the newspaper owner and a stranger some thought was the prince. The newspaperman, Horace Verne, had been shot, but not seriously.

They went to call on him at the office.

"Mr. Verne is not seeing anyone," a clerk told them.

They were allowed to send Verne a note, asking where the prince had gone. Verne scribbled an answer on the note: I don't know and I don't care.

Next they called on the livery stable owner. Often, they had learned, he knew the town's tales as well as any. The livery owner told them that two men had purchased a small coach and a horse to pull it. It was also common knowledge, he said, that the famous German prince who had been staying at the Harding Hotel was now gone from there.

Where had the prince gone?

"Well, the closest town's Wendover."

Horace Verne recovered quickly, enough to permit him to resume his duties at the paper. The shoulder inconvenienced him, it was annoying to have the arm in a sling, but it was worse to sit about at home doing nothing.

His first order of business was to prepare a scandalous attack on the prince, calling him various things such as a spy and a leech, living off the labor of his poor subjects. He conjured up a picture of a bloated, uncaring, scum-faced aristocrat who ground down his people, squeezing each penny from them, forcing them into the fields by means of bayonets. He also castigated the United States government for allowing this foreign maggot to travel the land in regal splendor.

He plastered the front page with it, a vicious tangle of lies and slander. Horace clothed himself in glorious white. He had met on the field of honor with the black prince's flunky, since the prince himself was too cowardly to risk his precious skin.

Next he exhorted all citizens to make the prince and his entourage unwelcome. "We do not need his useless kind in this country."

Horace doubled the usual printing run for the weekly and papers were sent to settlements they had never reached before.

Nate Tinkler and the Vinton brothers went directly to Wendover, traveling overland, not by the road. They could shave ten or fifteen miles off the journey, Nate said. He had been that way before.

The hotel clerk in Wendover easily recalled the hunting party and the man on crutches. However, he had to inform them it had departed. He had no idea where the party had gone. But a small coach had been left behind in the hotel stable. It was all he knew.

The three separated to ask questions in the saloons and the barbershop and livery. But no one in the town they could find had seen the hunting party ride out. They could have gone in any direction.

It was frustrating.

Ed and Will were unwilling to spend any of their slender funds for hotel rooms. Will located an abandoned shack on the outskirts of town and they moved in. Nate preferred to stay at the hotel.

"The closest town is Wendover," Karl Jung said musingly.

"That's north of here," Franz said, looking at a map.

"And they tell us the best hunting is in the north these days."

"Then let's go to Wendover."

Chapter Fourteen

IN Washington City, John Fleming received a copy of the Bonnet *Clarion* by special messenger. It was the edition that contained the scathing attack on Prince Knarig, and he was horrified and angered as he read it. It was all so unnecessary . . . and petulant.

His superiors were also vastly annoyed when he showed it to them. Unfortunately nothing could be done about it. The damage was already done; one cannot unbreak an egg.

In Fleming's opinion the government should stay out of the matter. Much as he would like to beat Horace Verne's butt, it might be best to ignore the attack.

The prince was no longer in Bonnet anyway, he told them. And it was to be hoped the people of the Reichenbach Embassy would not see the *Clarion*, which was, after all, a local weekly far out on the plains, with a small circulation.

However, Fleming's superiors still voiced their original objection to the prince's presence here at all, saying that he might be killed on United States soil and thus provoke an unpleasant international incident.

But nothing was done about that either.

It was a misty morning on the high plains when Charlie Bennett materialized in the ground fog and rode back to the main party, grinning widely.

"Buffalo," he said, when he reached them. "A small herd, not far away."

"Where?" Voss asked.

"Two miles into the wind." Charlie pointed.

Knarig spurred his horse. "Lead on, Mr. Bennett, please." He pulled his rifle from the boot and laid it across his thighs.

Laredo, out on a ridge to the south, saw Charlie return and talk to Voss and the prince. It was unusual, so it probably meant he had sighted buffalo—or Indians. But if it had been Indians he would have signaled him and Pete. Pete was on the ridge to the north; he would doubtless make the same assumption.

Laredo followed along, watching the guide. If Charlie had sighted buffalo they were probably in a hollow, grazing peacefully, with the wind blowing from them to the hunting party. He studied the darkening sky; it promised rain, but he hoped it would hold off a few hours till they made camp.

The ridge petered out in the next twenty minutes and he felt the first light drops of rain as he came down to the prairie grass. As he turned toward the party he saw Charlie halt suddenly. Then not far ahead he saw the herd—running northward.

There were only about two dozen head—and something had spooked them. They disappeared into the mists and the rain increased.

When Laredo joined them the prince was glum, but Voss swore great oaths, yelling at the gray skies, his frustration enormous. Charlie rode ahead and was gone half an hour. When he returned he shook his head, saying he could see no reason why they had stampeded.

"Except they been hunted t'death and prob'ly got the wind up. We can foller them."

Voss agreed and they went north for an hour till it began to get dark. There was a good stand of trees not far off and they pitched their tents under the branches as thunder rolled in the distance and a few spears of lightning flashed tentatively.

There was dry wood under the trees and they rigged a canvas shelter and made a fire. Winter was a-comin', Charlie said.

* * *

Karl Jung and Franz found rooms in a boardinghouse in Wendover and set about visiting the several saloons with the idea of asking about the prince. But they found to their surprise that the prince was already a subject of much debate and gossip, most concerning the attack on Knarig in the *Clarion*. The idlers were divided. Some thought the newspaperman's attack was justified; what the hell business did a foreign blue blood have in America anyway? Others thought it plainly showed what a mindless bigot Horace Verne was.

Karl and Franz stayed out of the arguments, but as they moved from one saloon to the next, listening and sipping beer, they became aware that another man was asking pointed questions about the prince. The questioner was a lean, wiry man who looked as if he did not have enormous patience. Karl overhead someone call him Nate.

He and Franz kept close watch on Nate, and when the lean man finally left the saloon they followed him in the dark. Nate was not sober and had no idea he was being tailed. He sang snatches of song to himself and he led them to a shack on the south edge of town, which he entered.

It was late but there was a candle or lamp burning inside the shack and, when Karl crawled close, he could hear voices. Someone was very unhappy with Nate because they had lost the prince!

The voice said loudly, "We come all this way and we ain't got a penny t'show fer it!"

"We will have, dammit! Hold your horses!"

There were growls and muttering; the voices were lowered and in a few moments Karl moved away, fearing discovery.

In their boardinghouse room he and Franz discussed the situation. The man called Nate was planning something with the men in the shack. Was it a robbery—or a kidnapping?

Franz thought they were planning to rob the hunting party. But Karl was not so sure—why shouldn't they try for big money?

Franz said, "What if they just want to kill the prince?"

"They don't even know him or anything about him!"

"But if they try to rob him there'll be a fight. Knarig won't give up easy."

Karl smiled. "Maybe they'll do our job for us. We ought to let them try."

The rain came down hard that night after they made camp under the trees. They were in three tents, the blue one for the prince.

But it rained all the next day, becoming a heavy downpour toward midday, barely tapering off as evening approached. It continued to rain the next morning and it was colder. Charlie thought it would snow soon. There was no question of their going after buffalo. They would have made scant progress, even Voss agreed. The earth was sodden and every tiny creek and stream was swollen and raging.

The storm lasted another day. The rain seemed to settle into a steady, hard, slanting downpour that pounded the ground. It let up after dark, drizzled for a bit, then everything was silent except for the constant dripping.

When they woke the following morning the land was white. It had snowed during the night; several inches covered everything.

The skies were clearing, and in the middle of the morning the sun came out. Charlie promised the snow would not last, and he was right. The sun warmed the land and the snow slowly melted away.

The map showed a tiny town not far to the east. It was called White Oak, and Voss suggested they go there. The prince was feeling the effects of the cold and damp—the leg was not completely healed. Knarig never complained, but his face was drawn and tight.

They broke camp and started out, with Charlie moving ahead to find the best trail. The town was farther away than it looked on the map. Laredo and Pete Torres rode far out on the flanks so they would not miss the burg, but they did not reach it that day. It clouded up in the late afternoon and misted for several hours, then started to rain again. Charlie found them an overhang above a raging stream, and they spent the night after coaxing wet wood to burn.

They reached White Oak late the next day. It was a settlement rather than a town, a few shacky buildings set down haphazardly astride the trail, devoid of paint or whitewash, looking lonely as the far hills. There was a store of sorts, connected to a barroom, but the place had no hotel, and no women.

The store owner allowed them to use an empty barn, so they were able to get out of the weather. The fact of their coming spread through the little place like wildfire and people stared at them covertly.

They had received copies of the Bonnet *Clarion*, and it took only a short time for them to realize that the object of Horace Verne's spleen was here—a real honest-to-God prince!

Emil erected the blue tent inside the barn so Knarig would have privacy and this, when it was noticed, caused much attention and prattle. Imagine someone pitching a tent inside a barn! What kinds of crazy things did foreigners do?

Ernst Krone had come from the old country with his wife, Katy, and settled in White Oak because his cousin lived there, and because land was his for the taking.

He had left Germany for a variety of reasons: the excesses of the ruling class, the burden of taxes, oppressive laws, the years one had to spend in the military. . . . He had become a member of a protest group as a young man and had spent two years at hard labor because of his actions.

Released from prison, he had been constantly watched and he knew suspicion would be upon him the rest of his life. Ernst was not a man who bent easily, and the prison had not broken him. But the authorities made it plain that greater punishments were ahead if he returned to his insurgent course.

Katy suggested an alternative. Pick up and follow his cousin to America!

Ernst thought about it for half a year as he saved every bit of money that came his way. His cousin wrote that land to farm was free and he could think as he pleased. So when he had the fare for himself and Katy, they made the long voyage.

That had been seven years ago.

Now he had a farm that supported them. He had milk cows, a small herd of sheep, chickens, a vegetable garden, and he paid no taxes and bowed his head to no man. The government did not conscript men into the army. He was truly free for the fist time in his life.

And then this German prince showed up with his fine clothes, his servants, and entourage—and pitched his tent in a barn!

In a mounting rage, Ernst listened to the prattle in Grogan's deadfall. The prince, it was said, was hunting buffalo. Everyone knew the buffalo had been hunted out; it was a measure of the European's stupidity. No one had seen a buffalo near White Oak in a decade.

Ernst was thirty-four now, a stocky, hard-muscled man who was generally liked by his neighbors; he was generous, hard-working and helpful. He minded his own business and had wanted to forget the old country—until now. He brooded about the prince. What they had done to him in Germany still rankled. How could he forget those years at hard labor?

When he muttered about it to Katy she replied that those days were behind them. They were secure now. No one could pull him back across the ocean to serve in the army or to grind him down in other ways. They were free. Forget about the prince; he will soon be gone.

She was right, of course. The Prussians could not reach him here. But he could reach one of them! He could even the score—just a little bit.

He had an old Sharps rifle he'd traded for several years past to use in hunting deer. He took it to the shed behind the house and cleaned it carefully. The army had taught him to zero in a rifle and he had done it with the Sharps out in the fields. It fired about two inches to the left at two hundred yards.

It was raining again lightly, and with it a cold mist drifted across the trees and fields. Smoke trailed from the distant chimneys, curling and shredding into nothingness.

Laredo thrust hands deep into his pockets and hunched

his shoulders as he stood in the doorway of the barn. He asked Pete: "Is there any way someone could have tracked us here?"

Pete shook his head. "I don't see how. We didn't know we were coming here ourselves. And nobody tracked us through that storm." He glanced back at the closed blue tent. "His honor is prob'ly asleep again."

The prince spent a great deal of time in the tent. What else could he be doing other than sleeping? Charlie Bennett thought Knarig preferred it to mixing with commoners. Of course Voss said the prince was resting the leg.

Laredo said, "Charlie says it'll stop raining in a day or so. Then we'll have about two weeks before the snows come."

"How long will it take us to get back to St. Louis?"

"Probably a week."

Pete rolled a brown cigarette. "Well, if Charlie's right, this hunting trip is about over for the year."

"Don't be too sure." Laredo sighed. "We may all be on snowshoes yet."

Pete groaned.

Grogan's was the only saloon in the little settlement. It was a dimly lighted narrow room smelling of oil, tobacco, and other things all mixed into one. There was a long plank bar with a step in front in lieu of rail, and there were a few rickety tables, chairs, and benches. It looked very seedy.

Grogan himself looked just as seedy and unkempt. He had only one leg, claiming to have lost the other in the war. He hobbled about on one crutch. The idea of a foreign prince in White Oak was obviously fascinating to him and he was eager for details, setting up free beer for Charlie, who was the only one who obliged him.

Laredo and Pete listened as Charlie unreeled long, involved stories concerning Knarig, stories that Charlie was making up as he went along—with Grogan swallowing them whole. Grogan had not the slightest conception of a prince, how he lived or talked or whatever, and he was willing to believe anything.

Pete was somehow able to listen to this finely spun nonsense with a straight face, but Laredo had to slip outside now and then for relief.

The very first day there was a break in the weather, Colonel Voss sent Charlie out to scout the hills and badlands to the north. If there were buffalo anywhere within a hundred miles it was likely to be there, so said the hangers-on at the bar.

It was getting on toward midday when Prince Knarig came to the entrance of the barn with a rifle in his hands, examining it in the new sunlight. The rain had gone, though there were puddles everywhere and the trees were dripping.

He had just pulled the hammer back when the shot came.

The heavy bullet hit the rifle barrel a few inches from the prince's fingers. It knocked the rifle from his hands and sent him spinning. The report of the sniper's rifle was heard a second later.

Voss, inside the barn, came running, drawing his revolver. Several hundred yards away, through the trees, a man on a horse was galloping off toward the east. He was too far for pistol shooting, but Voss shook the revolver at him. He disappeared in a moment.

Then Voss ran to the prince. "Are you hurt, Cesar?"

"I . . . I don't think so. . . ." Knarig got to his feet. He was bruised but otherwise unhurt. He had been lucky; the rifle barrel had saved him. The bullet might have gone into his heart.

Voss pulled him away from the doorway in case there were others waiting their chance, but no more shots came. Pete had been napping in the back of the barn; he quickly saddled a horse and went riding in the direction taken by the unknown rifleman.

Laredo was in the general store discussing the weather with the proprietor when they heard the shot. But shots were not all that uncommon, and neither of them thought anything of it, not one single shot.

But when he returned to the barn and heard the news, he,

too, saddled his horse and rode after Pete. Had they been tracked down after all?

He joined Pete several miles outside of town and the other shook his head. "I followed his tracks but he lost me. He knows every inch of this ground." Pete fiddled with a sack of Blackwell's. "I suspicion it was somebody who lives here."

Laredo was surprised. "How could the prince have an enemy in a little burg in the middle of nowhere! None of these people ever saw or heard of him before!"

Pete made an offhand gesture. "I know it's peculiar, but let me show you something." He motioned and they rode back a short way. He pointed out how the sniper had taken advantage of a section of hard ground to lose a pursuer.

"If he did not know every foot of this ground he wouldn't have known to come this exact way."

"Maybe he was lucky."

"Not a bit of it. The tracks curved from the vicinity of the barn and came directly here. He was a man in a hurry, remember. But he didn't ride in a straight line or he'd have missed this section. I think he planned it ahead of time."

Laredo gazed at the sky, dark at the horizons; it smelled like rain. He sighed deeply. "Then you think it was someone who shot at him only because he's a prince?"

"Maybe because of what he represents—yes. Isn't that possible?"

"What if Horace Verne has a relative here who is willing to take up his fight?"

Pete laughed and lit the cigarette. "I doubt if Horace's mother would take up his fight."

They turned the horses to go back. Pete was probably right. It could be that someone who lived in White Oak had emigrated from Reichenbach years ago and still held grudges. Such things could burrow deep into a man's soul.

But how could they investigate every family in the little settlement?

Pete's thoughts paralleled his own. "It would take too long to track him down—and there's no law in White Oak to help."

People would not stand for strangers questioning them,

either. Then they would have more than one single sniper on their hands.

Laredo glanced at the sky again. Left by himself he would track the man down, but he and Pete had a responsibility. It might be best to move on—get the prince out of danger.

When they returned to the barn he mentioned it to Voss, who was in instant agreement.

But Knarig was not.

He would remain until Charlie Bennett got back, he told them. Then they would continue the hunt. The sniper was beneath his notice.

And so the matter rested.

Chapter Fifteen

AN official envelope was brought round to him: John Fleming was asked to attend a meeting in the office of the Secretary of State, Mr. Peabody. Attached to the memo was a note asking Fleming not to smoke. Mr. Peabody was afflicted by cigars.

The meeting was held in a large, wood-paneled room that was dominated by a huge oval-shaped table and sixteen thickly padded chairs. One of the secretary's aides showed Fleming to a chair near the end of the table, where two others were already seated.

"I think you know Mr. Rennet and Mr. Adams . . . ?"

"Hello," Fleming said, reaching for a cigar, remembering at the last instant. They both smiled at the gesture; the aide brought a tray containing a silver pot and cups. "Coffee, gentleman. The secretary will be here in a moment."

Adams poured into the cups and the secretary entered. Everyone stood and Peabody smiled at Fleming. "Good of you to come, John."

Peabody was always polite. Fleming murmured something and sat again.

Peabody had a packet of notebooks and papers. He laid out a few pencils, fiddled with a notebook, and said, "It's about that Reichenbach prince, John. We've had a change of minds."

"Oh, is that so, sir?"

"We let the fellow go into the interior on a hunting trip—as you well know."

"Yes."

"We've had a flood of cables from Reichenbach. Apparently the reigning prince is pretty nearly on his deathbed, poor fellow. And Prince Knarig, the one who's out hunting, will succeed him."

Fleming made noises in his throat.

Peabody picked up a pencil and looked at it hard. "Do you know where Knarig is now, John?"

Fleming shook his head. "I don't, sir."

Adams spoke sharply. "Aren't you responsible for him?"

Peabody tapped the pencil. "Wait a moment, Fred. Nobody is *responsible* for him. The prince pretty well does as he damn pleases. Isn't that right, John?"

"Unfortunately yes, sir. We were told in the beginning that he was hardheaded and stubborn."

The secretary studied his notes. "That newspaper article that came out against him was from a little town called Bonnet?"

"That's right, sir. But the prince left there before the article appeared. As you know, I have men with him and they report by wire whenever they can."

Adams said, "I didn't know you had men with him."

"Yes, two operatives from the Tanner Organization. Their orders are to protect the prince if possible. We have learned that members of the Reichenbach protest people are actively seeking to do him harm."

"Yes, we know about that," Peabody said.

"My men will report whenever possible, sir. Unfortunately very few towns in the West are on the telegraph and the West is a vast area. The mails are out of the question. A letter might take a month to arrive."

Peabody frowned. "This entire Reichenbach Affair has become a nuisance. We cannot have European princes running about our country with gangs of men after them. It simply will not do! I've discussed this matter with the president, and we agree, something must be done immediately. The prince must be recalled."

"Deported, sir?"

Peabody looked aghast. "Oh my goodness, no! Please don't use that word! No, no, no. We will gently escort him out, bowing and scraping—but out he will go. We do not want him to be killed on United States soil!"

Fleming nodded, aching for a cigar. "I understand, sir."

"Please attempt to get in touch with your two men. Perhaps you can wire all likely towns. I will see that army posts are alerted. Perhaps a cavalry patrol will turn them up and bring them in."

"Very well, sir. However, as I said, the prince is stubborn as h— very stubborn. What if he will not obey orders?"

Peabody sighed. "I am sorry to say we must let Garrett and Torres use force. It has been decided to send him back to Reichenbach. We will wash our hands of him." He gathered his notes. "Do you have any questions, John?"

Fleming shook his head. "None at all, sir." He rose as Peabody got up and went out.

Charlie Bennett was gone nearly a week, and the weather had been fair. He had ridden a huge circle, he told them on returning. He had seen one band of Indians but had stayed hidden and they had passed him by. He had seen grazing buffalo, "Not many, but a few," and could lead them back. "But they looked a mite scrawny."

Knarig decided they would go at once.

Because of the mysterious sniper they departed from the little settlement long after dark—the prince left his crutches behind—and rode northwest until dawn before halting to make camp, and breakfast.

Nate Tinkler and the Vinton brothers stayed indoors during the rainstorms. When the sun came out again Nate convinced them to head north, saying that was the way the prince's party had been pointing. It was the only fact they knew.

Ed Vinton growled and kicked the ground like a bull, but had to admit the only other choice was to give it all up.

Nate told him, "You give it up now and you got nothing for all your trouble."

"And if we go on, and git more nothing—it's still nothing!"

"But at least we got a chance at real money . . . enough to set us up for years."

It was the "real money" argument that won the day for Nate. Neither of the Vintons had any money at all. They were poor as lizards, so Nate advanced them a few dollars and they agreed to start north next morning.

But after Nate had left, Ed frowned at the money he had given them—three dollars. He sighed and looked at his brother. "We ain't been so poor in a coon's age."

Will pulled at his chin. "What you sayin', Ed?"

"I'm sayin' there's ways to git money." He patted his revolver.

Will grinned, showing big yellow teeth. "Now you talkin' my langridge. What's your idee?"

"Hell, what we done before. We hang around one of them saloons tonight and see who comes out."

They had done exactly that in half a dozen towns. They had never made much money at it, but a dollar was a dollar. Will pulled his Colt, opened the loading gate, and examined the brass.

They spent thirty cents each for fine meals in the town's best restaurant, had a couple of drinks each in the saloon next door, then sat in tilted-back chairs near the hotel to watch the activity on the street. Their bellies were full, for once that month.

When it got full dark they went back to the shack and rolled in their blankets for a few hours.

The town was mostly asleep when they came out and walked along the main street, approaching the Senate Saloon. A yellow glow of light came from the batwing doors, along with the sounds of a fiddle and piano and several wavering but eager voices.

Ed looked over the top of the door; the saloon was not crowded—a dozen to fifteen men were gabbing at the bar or playing cards at the tables, most in store suits.

He nodded to Will and they took up station, one on either side of the door, not too close to it. Each man arranged his wipe so it could easily be drawn up over his nose to conceal his face.

They waited. The first man out of the saloon stumbled on the boardwalk and nearly fell to the street, swearing. Ed motioned to let him go; he did not look as if he had a copper in his kick.

Then a ragged-looking man came out, talking to himself. They let him pass by. It was a long wait till the next man. He was wearing a bowler hat and had a pale, fancy vest under his coat. Ed nodded and pulled up his wipe. This one looked like money.

Bowler Hat walked by Will, probably not seeing him as he was flat up against the wall in the dark. He went to one of a dozen horses along the hitch rack and Will followed. Ed circled into the street. They would each approach him from opposite sides.

When Will got close he yanked back the hammer on his Colt, *click-clack*.

Bowler Hat heard it, turned, and instantly produced a derringer. As he cocked it, Will fired twice. Bowler Hat was pushed back violently and went to his knees. The derringer dropped into the dust. The hat came off and rolled onto the street as the victim fell on his side and rolled onto his back. The horses shied, pulling at reins.

Ed ran to the man and frisked him quickly, coming up with a wallet.

Will said, "He had a gun, Ed. . . ."

"Git outa here!" Ed pointed, and they ran along the street and ducked into the space between two buildings as men spilled from the saloon.

No one gave chase—they had not been seen—and they returned to the shack without challenge. Ed scratched a match and put it to a candle. The wallet contained seventeen dollars and some papers they burned, not being able to read them. Ed went outside and flung the leather wallet into a field.

He was annoyed that Will had shot the man, but Will protested he'd had no choice.

"He had a gun, dammit! I woulda had a bullet in the belly in another second!"

"All right, all right, but they going to be lookin' at strangers in town. No telling who that hombre was."

"He was prob'ly a gambler. Looked like one anyhow."

"Well, if he was, maybe nobody will worry too much." Ed fingered the money. "Not much in 'is kick for a gambler to be packin'."

Will giggled. "He was down on 'is luck."

"He sure'n hell was." Ed bit his lip. "We oughta git out tonight."

"Outa town?"

"It'd be safer. But we got to let Nate know." Ed scowled. "If we go to the hotel after him now, it'll cause talk."

"But if we mosey into town in the morning . . ."

Ed grinned. "That's right. We'd just be strangers comin' in. How the hell would we know about the shootin' the night before?" He looked hard at his brother. "Long's we keep our mouths shut."

Will was aggrieved. "Don't worry 'bout me!"

"All right. But you say nothing, hear?"

Will glowered and Ed said, "That's what we'll do. Git out tonight and come in t'morra. Git your possibles together."

When Nate went down to breakfast the next morning he heard about the shooting. An ordinary shooting didn't cause that much talk, but it was all over town that Judge Elland had been gunned down and robbed in the street as he came out of the Senate Saloon.

The town council met at once and offered five hundred dollars reward for the killer. But no one had seen it done. The judge's widow increased the amount by a hundred.

As Nate ate his steak and eggs he thought of Ed and Will Vinton. It was exactly the exercise they were good at. He knew for a fact they had done the same thing several times before. It could almost be considered their trademark. He wondered if they were still at the shack.

When he stepped out of the restaurant three men intercepted him; all wore star badges: deputy. One asked, "You stayin' at the hotel, mister?"

"Yes I am." One of the deputies disarmed him, looked at his pistol, and smelled the barrel.

He shook his head. "Ain't been fired or cleaned in a while." He gave the gun back. "What you doing in town?"

"Passin' through. I live in Hendon. This about that shooting?"

"Yeah." They motioned him on. He watched them stop another citizen, then he went for his horse in the stable. He rode to the shack to find it empty. The Vintons had flown.

He was positive then it had been them. The damn fools had to pick a judge! Nate swore, blew out his breath, and went back to the hotel. What the hell should he do now? He'd never in the world be able to kidnap the prince single-handed.

As he approached the hotel he saw there was a small crowd in front of it. Men were standing around, talking, spitting, and looking. Nate edged close and saw the same three deputies. They were questioning Ed and Will Vinton. Ed glanced at him without a change of expression. He and his brother had just come into town, he told the lawmen. "What's all the fuss?"

"Judge got shot last night." One deputy said to Will, "Your gun been fired recent."

Will shrugged. "I fired at a coyote yestiddy. I didn't know I'd be ast about it."

"Let's see what you both got in your pockets."

The brothers turned them out. Nate saw they had more than the three dollars he'd given them, but they had no papers of any kind, not even letters. They had nothing that had belonged to the judge.

A deputy asked, "What you doing in town?"

"Ridin' through is all. We never shot nobody. Hell, never been here b'fore." Ed's face was as innocent as the dawn, and Will was as wide-eyed as a moo cow.

The deputies let them go and continued questioning others.

Nate put up his horse and walked to the nearest saloon. Ed and Will were already there. With a grin, Ed bought the drinks.

Chapter Sixteen

ONCE every ten days to two weeks, copies of far eastern newspapers, such as the *New York Times*, the *Kansas City Tattler*, and the *Chicago Post*, filtered through to Wendover. Karl Jung bought a *Plaindealer* that was only two weeks old and sat down to read it.

On an inside page he discovered the heading: FOREIGN PRINCE TO LEAVE COUNTRY. The item said that the State Department was asking Prince Knarig of Reichenbach to return home at the earliest opportunity. The reigning prince, Lothar, was seriously ill, and the Foreign Minister had made the request since Knarig was next in line to the throne.

But Knarig had not been found so that he could receive the message. It was said he was somewhere on the western plains, out of touch with civilization.

Karl said to Franz, "This means we have less time than I thought. When the prince is given the message he will have to return, and if he reaches Reichenbach . . ." Karl sighed. "Then we will have lost."

"But we don't know where he is! No one knows, apparently. What can we do?"

"We cannot stay here doing nothing! We may move the wrong way, but at least let us move!"

"Very well. What do you have in mind?"

The morning of the third day since they'd left White Oak behind, it began to rain again. The hunting party stayed in the three tents and let it pour. Toward afternoon it became a steady, hard rain, as if it had decided to continue forever.

Charlie Bennett suggested to Voss that the party return east for the year. Buffalo would be harder and harder to find—if they ever found any. They would be well advised to try again in the spring.

Voss relayed the suggestion to the prince and it was turned down.

That evening the rain let up suddenly and it did not rain again. The morning dawned overcast and threatening, but the sun came out after an hour and they broke camp. With Charlie as point and with Laredo and Pete far out to the sides, they went on northwest, hoping to catch sight of grazing animals.

It drizzled, putting out the sun, and once a hard rain squall came sweeping down upon them and passed by in half an hour. Laredo walked his horse through it and came along a ridge to find Charlie waiting for him.

He pointed to the south. "Seems like I seen two fellers thataway just as the rain cleared."

Laredo got out the binoculars and scanned the horizon. "How far?"

"A mile'r two. Just had a fast look, then they was gone."

"D'you think they saw you?"

"Hard to say." Charlie shrugged.

"Well, I'd better have a look."

"You better go with Pete." Charlie turned and waved and Pete, half a mile away, turned his mount instantly.

They rode south, separating to cover more ground, staying within sight of each other as it began to rain again. Laredo flushed out a flock of quail, but they saw nothing else that moved.

It rained harder and it was difficult to see for any distance. After several miles Laredo signaled Pete and they halted in a copse of trees where there was some shelter. The men Charlie had seen were doubtless holed up somewhere, too, and it would only be by enormous luck that he and Pete would locate them.

The rain continued through the night, only drizzling at

times, and by morning a feathery snow was falling, powdering the land with patches of white.

They rode a wide circle, looking for tracks, and saw none. The men Charlie had seen had disappeared without a trace.

"Probably pilgrims," Pete said. "If they turned south when Charlie noticed them, they could be fifty miles gone by now."

Laredo scratched his throat and studied the sky. "I say, let's go back. It's going to keep on snowing."

"And the wind is coming up. . . ."

They turned north again and before they had gone a mile they were in a blizzard. Heads down, they walked the horses slowly heading into the storm, wipes pulled up over their faces. It was cold and getting colder.

When they figured they had gone far enough, they began to look for tracks. Pete pulled his pistol and sent four shots into the dark, swirling sky.

They heard no answer.

"Somebody's lost," Laredo shouted over the wind. "Either us or them."

Pete pointed. "Let's go on west. They should be holed up somewhere."

In the next few miles they saw no one. The snow turned to sleet and the wind pounded them. When they came to a rocky hill with a stand of trees on the east side, they ducked under the thick branches, happy to get out of the cutting wind. They had no great fear that the prince and Emil would suffer in the storm. Charlie Bennett would see they rode it out.

But, Pete said, they really ought to be heading back to St. Louis.

They were moving single file, beating their way through thick, snow-laden brush. The prince happened to be in the rear, and a wild bird—perhaps a turkey—fluttered up in front of his horse. The mount shied, stumbled, and suddenly jumped into a headlong run, galloping off to the right in the midst of the blizzard.

The organ-toned wind covered the sounds, and even Emil

did not notice for a full minute that the prince was no longer behind him.

Knarig, an excellent horseman, let the animal have its head for a few moments, then attempted to regain control, without success. He swore, trying to pull the horse's head around, but the frightened mount turned tail to the wind and ran with the bit in its teeth and Knarig could only keep his seat and shout.

He did not realize for a moment that he was riding with the wind rather than into it. The galloping animal was carrying him away very fast! He got his revolver out and fired into the sky—the sound only made the horse go faster! And the shots seemed flat and toneless to him—would Voss and the others hear them? He emptied the pistol and thrust it back into his belt.

Shaking its head, the horse ran north, wild-eyed, as Knarig gradually regained control. Lightning flashed in the distance and snow changed to rain. He managed to turn the horse and before he realized it the animal was charging into a raging stream. Icy water splashed over him as it slowed the horse.

Across the stream he came to a marsh, hock-deep and weedy. The rain hammered down and thunder rolled out of the west—was it a new storm? It was getting dark. He had to go back across the stream again. He put spurs to the tiring horse and headed for the white water.

The horse struggled mightily but was swept downstream. Knarig fought to stay aboard, but he was thrust off the animal's back by the force of water. He went under, then flailed, kicking with all his strength until he felt bottom. The heedless stream flung him up on a curve like so much driftwood, pounding him a bit. He crawled up onto a grassy patch, chest heaving.

The horse was nowhere to be seen.

It was raining hard and the entire area was lighted up for a second by a jagged streak of lightning. He got to his feet, regaining his breath. He was soaked through and cold; he had to get moving. It was too cold to stand still.

He had lost everything: blanket, roll, canteen, rifle . . . but he had matches in a screwtop tin container. If he was lucky, they were still dry.

The storm came out of the west, so he headed in that

direction. He had heard Charlie Bennett say, "the quickest way west is into the wind." Pulling his coat tightly about him, he hunched his shoulders and went doggedly on.

In an hour he came to some low sandy cliffs. At their foot stood a great tangle of brush and trees. He pushed his way in among them and found the ground dry. He was out of the wind! With his knife he dug and scraped a hole as he had seen Charlie do. He put tiny twigs and dead leaves into it and opened the tin container. The matches were dry! He said a little prayer to the God of hunters as he scratched one and lighted the kindling.

In a few minutes he had a good fire going and had to hustle to feed it. He had no food at all; he was ravenous. But he was out of the storm; his back was cold but his front was warm.

Events had taken a disgusting turn, and for one of the few times in his life he had no power to control them. He had to accept his fate. How long could he last in the wilderness?

He collected a large pile of wood. He would keep the fire going all night. Turning about, he gradually dried his clothes and was more comfortable. But he could not simply sit still and feed the fire. His military training had taught him a few things. He cut stout branches with the hunting knife and in a few hours had built a sort of lean-to shelter that kept him much warmer.

He still had his pistol and thought of shooting a rabbit—but he saw none at all. At any rate, he had never skinned one and had no idea how to go about it. People had always done that for him.

He kept the fire going through the night, though he fell asleep several times and woke barely in time to lay twigs on glowing embers and build it up again. In the morning he was tired and stiff and the hurt leg was beginning to ache. He told himself he was a soldier. He could stand a little pain and a little hunger.

The storm was fitful. The rain pattered down and the wind howled through the treetops. Knarig debated his choices. He could continue walking westward or he could stay where he was. If he started walking he might find himself on the open plain with no shelter at all, and it might be easy to pass Voss and the others and never know it.

On the other hand there was plenty of wood for the fire, and surely the others would find him soon.

He decided to stay.

That afternoon the rain became a drizzle and the wind slackened. He had a beltful of cartridges so he began firing one about every half hour. The sound should carry in the clear air. . . .

Ernst Krone quickly discovered that the prince's party had left the settlement. He had a decision to make: should he ignore his feelings or should he take action again? He did not ponder the question long—he was a stubborn man, and singleminded. Without saying a word to anyone he saddled a horse and followed their tracks, his Sharps rifle across his thighs.

He told himself the mere fact of the prince's appearance in White Oak was a sign. It was almost as if the Creator had annointed him and sent him to avenge the subjugated peoples of the earth. He would never forgive himself if he passed up this opportunity.

But the storm caught him and swept away the tracks he followed. He wandered for hours before he came to a rude shelter in a windrow of fallen trees. He got down, managed a tiny fire, and made it through the night—then waited patiently till the storm began to pass to the east.

He had lost the party and knew that the chances of finding it again were very slim. He went on slowly; he had food for several days but little desire to spend many nights on the open plains.

And as he thought glumly about returning to White Oak, he heard the shot.

He was startled. The shot seemed to come from an area south of him and he rode that way. Was someone hunting? He moved very slowly, watchful as a timber wolf.

A second shot, a half hour later, surprised him. It came from a tangled stand of trees to his front. Dismounting at the edge of the trees he slipped in among them, smelling smoke.

Someone had a fire going. He moved like an Indian and caught sight of a shelter made of branches. He lay flat and crawled forward, inching along.

A man came into view and knelt to place sticks on the fire. He looked like an ordinary pilgrim, probably someone waiting out the storm.

Krone got to his feet. He said, "Hello there."

The man jumped and grabbed at a pistol.

Krone said, "Don't shoot." He stepped into the clear, arms extended to show he had no weapon. The other nodded and shoved the pistol back into his belt. He was young, no more than twenty-five, Krone thought, and his clothes were wrinkled and dirty; he was unshaven and looked very tired.

The man said, "Who are you?"

"My name is Ernst Krone. I was caught by the storm."

"Yes, so was I. I lost my horse. Are you on foot also?"

"No. My horse is back there." Krone moved his head. "Are you traveling alone?"

"No. I got separated from the rest of my party."

"Ahhh. That's why you were firing."

"Yes."

Krone studied the other. He was part of a group? Maybe the prince's hunting party. He asked, "What is your name?"

"Nicholas Monat."

"You are not a German?"

The other smiled and shrugged lightly. "No, I am not."

"Have you eaten? I have some food in my saddlebags."

"You are very kind."

Krone nodded and went back to bring the horse close. Then they sat by the fire to share the food.

Chapter Seventeen

KNARIG was astonished to see the man who had appeared suddenly from nowhere. His name, he said, was Ernst Krone. He looked to be a farmer, but why was he out here in the storm?

Prince Knarig had used several names in the past when he wished to conceal his identity. He gave one of them to Krone, Nicholas Monat. The farmer seemed satisfied; he had a rather thick German accent, but he seemed a good fellow, and best of all, he had food.

He was also very curious about Monat's party.

"We were hunting," Knarig said offhandedly.

"Ahhh. And is there a prince in the party?"

"Yes. . . ."

Krone's eyes blazed. "He is a German?"

"No," Knarig said softly. "He is from Reichenbach."

The farmer was astonished. "From Reichenbach!"

"Yes."

"But . . . but, I saw the newspaper! It said—"

"Yes. We saw it, too. It was wrong. The editor did not bother with facts."

Krone stared at the other, digesting the news. Knarig thought he did not want to believe it—for whatever reason. Finally Krone said, "The prince—he is a pompous, arrogant person?"

Was this man one of those conspirators? He did not look like anything but a farmer, but what was he doing out in the storm? And he was well armed. . . . Knarig frowned; he must be on his guard against treachery. "No, he is not."

The stranger looked unhappy at this. In a moment he said. "But you—what do you do?"

Knarig shrugged. "I am only a servant." Could he carry it off?

"Ahhh. You have been with the prince a long time?"

"Yes. A very long time."

"Does he treat you well?"

Knarig shrugged again. "Yes, well enough."

The other sighed deeply and a faraway look came into his eyes. "It was different in Germany. I was happy to leave and I will never go back."

Knarig managed a smile. "Reichenbach is not Germany."

"No, of course not." Krone sighed again. "Of course not." They finished the food and the farmer rose, looking at the clearing sky. "I think you will be found soon if you remain here. Build up the fire and send a thick column of smoke into the sky."

"Yes, I will."

"If I see your party I will send them here."

"You are very kind."

Ernst Krone mounted and looked down at him. "If I were you I would leave the prince's service and settle down here in America. A man can acquire land for the asking and make a good life for himself."

Knarig smiled. "I will think about it."

•

The hunting party was scattered. Emil was the first to realize the prince was not in view. He shouted to Voss and instantly set off on the back trail with Voss in pursuit.

Charlie Bennett, Laredo, and Pete Torres heard the shouts and halted. They looked at each other in wonder, then Laredo turned his mount and spurred after the others. He caught up to Voss in several miles.

"What is it?"

Voss called back, "The prince! He's gone!"

Gone? Where the hell would he go?

"His horse ran away with him," Emil yelled, making a helpless gesture.

"Did you see him go?" Laredo demanded.

"No."

"Then he could have gone in any direction!"

Voss reined in, glaring at Emil. "That's right. How did you get ahead of him?"

"I don't know, sir. He fell back—I hardly noticed in the storm—and then he was suddenly gone."

Voss swore, squinting into the wind.

"We can't separate," Laredo said, "not now—or we'll all get lost."

But Voss was in no mood to stand still. He roared at them to follow and set out, galloping the horse with the wind. They could do nothing but follow.

By nightfall they had not come upon Knarig.

They spent a miserable cold night and searched all the next day. Voss was like a grizzly who has lost her cub. He hated to halt the search at sundown, and he was the first up in the morning, eager to be off.

It was a fair morning; the storm had passed and a weak sun came out, smiling down on a wet, sodden world.

When they came to a higher, pointed hill, different from the others close by, Laredo suggested they separate, search north and south of the hill and return to it by dark—or sooner if they were successful.

Voss agreed at once.

He, Charlie, and Emil went north. Laredo and Pete turned south and in the first hour came upon a raging stream that flowed generally south. They followed it, well apart to cover more ground.

Nate Tinkler and the Vinton Brothers weathered the storm. As they started out, with the sun making a welcome appearance, Will Vinton noticed the distant smoke.

He pointed it out. "That's not a campfire—too much smoke."

"Maybe it's a signal," Nate replied. "Let's ease up on it and see what's doing."

The smoke came from a tangled wood a mile or more to the east. When they walked their horses into it from three sides they found a single man there, feeding the fire from a pile of broken branches. He had no horse and was astonished to see them.

"We seen your smoke," Nate explained, leaning on the pommel. "You afoot?"

"Yes, I lost my horse in the stream during the storm."

His English was too perfect. Nate asked suspiciously, "What's your name?"

"Nicholas Monat. What's yours?"

"Nate Tinkler." Nate studied the man; dirty and weathered clothes, but underneath the grime they were not ordinary dry goods duds. His boots, though scuffed and muddy, were not cheapies either. And he did not look like a farmer or a simple pilgrim. . . .

Nate dismounted. "You out here alone?"

"I got separated from my party."

Nate glanced at Ed, who smiled. Ed was onto it. This man was not what he seemed.

Nate said, "I don't think you're no Nicholas Monat. I think you're the prince." He made a sign to Ed and, stepping forward, took the man's revolver as Ed held his arms.

"Jesus!" Will said. "He's the prince?"

"Sure he is. Got separated from them others." He grinned at Knarig. "Own up. You're that German prince, huh?"

"I'm not a German," Knarig growled. "The newspapers were wrong."

Nate was suddenly all business. "Put that goddamn fire out. Stop the smoke." He watched the brothers kick dirt over the fire. "Let's get a-going. Prince, you ride up behint Willie."

"Where we going, Nate?" Ed asked.

"Back to Bonnet, to the Ferguson place—for now. Hurry it up."

It was a vast, empty land. Laredo and Pete rode half a mile apart, making a large sweep to return to the pointed hill by sundown. Voss and the others came in shortly after, having seen no one.

Voss was irritable and grumpy, tending to swear at Emil for invisible reasons. In his eyes, Emil had let His Highness get away.

They camped at the base of the hill, each man keeping to himself. The tension was thick. Voss walked out beyond the firelight and remained for more than an hour, muttering to himself and kicking the sod. They all knew what he was thinking. He would have to make a report to Lothar. The prince was his responsibility. His alone. He might shout at Emil, but when he stood before Lothar, all the blame would be his. Emil's name would not be mentioned. He would take the blame and his career would be over.

If they did not find the prince—alive.

They came upon the dead horse next day. Pete found it on the bank of the still-surging stream. The animal had obviously been swept downstream by the hard current and pounded to death on rocks. There was no trace of Knarig.

When Voss was summoned, he ordered them south along the stream at once. Perhaps the prince had been able to fight his way out of the mainstream and was still alive.

Perhaps.

A few miles downstream the water widened and became shallow, flowing over a sandy bottom. There was no evidence that Knarig had come this far.

What to do now?

The weather was holding, cold but fair; the skies were clear. Voss decided they would go back north again and spread the search. "He has to be somewhere!"

They rode north along the stream, their last contact with Knarig. Maybe they would see something they had missed. . . .

It took them a week to return to Bonnet. They kept off all roads and trails and made various detours, moving slowly because one horse had to carry double.

The Vintons wanted to take the road south from Wendover, saying they could easily bushwhack an unwary traveler and get a horse, but Nate was more cautious. He had the prince now, and he did not intend to lose him by some freak encounter.

When at last, one afternoon, they came in sight of the shacks of Bonnet, they halted for nightfall. Ed Vinton went to scout the old Ferguson place, in case some drifter had moved in while they were gone.

But no one had. He returned and led them around the town to the house and barn. It was three or four miles from the edge of town in a clump of trees. The road that had once led to it was overgrown and could hardly be called a road anymore. It was one of the things Nate liked about the place. There was nothing there anyone would want.

The old house had nothing over the windows and was filthy and musty inside. The barn was in better condition. They put the prince in a stall with his feet tied and made a tiny fire, settling in for the night.

Nate and the Vintons held a council of war. Now that the prince was actually in their hands, ransoming him did not seem as easy as it had before. There were certain problems.

"We can't send a telegram from Bonnet," Nate said. "They'll know where it come from, and they'll surround the town and turn us up."

"Then what can we do?" Will asked. "Post a letter?"

"Hell, no. That'd take a year."

Ed said, "Go to another town?"

"That's another thing," Nate replied. "Most of the towns with a telegraph is on the railroad. What worries me is, after we send the first wire, maybe they'll get smart and put men in ever' telegraph office from here to Kansas City."

"Could they do that? You tryin' to call this-here thing off?" Will asked.

"Hell no, I ain't callin' nothing off. But we don't want t'be caught neither. We's going to have to put the blue blood somewhere safe and tell them where he is after they pay us."

"After we're long gone," Ed agreed. "I like the sound o'that. But someone got to stay with him till then. You don't figger to let them find 'is body, huh?"

Nate shook his head. "No, I don't. If we shoot 'im it'll

go hard on us *if* they catch us. We'd be smart to keep him alive.''

Ed nodded, looking across the dark barn to where the prince was curled up in the stall. His murder would really raise the roof!

Nate rolled a cigarette and struck a match on his boot heel. ''Best thing is for you two to stay here with him. I'll ride down to some burg on the railroad—''

''That'll take a week!''

''Yeah, I know, but it got to be done. I'll send a wire to the gover'ment tellin' them we got the prince and we want one hunnerd thousand for him.''

Ed frowned. ''The telegraph operator's gonna read the message.''

''Can't help that. I'll send it when nobody's around. He won't get outa my sight.''

''What about a reply?''

''I'll wait for it.''

''But soon's them gover'ment people reads the message ain't they going to put the cavalry on your tail?''

Nate made a face. ''Hell, that'll take a month. I'll be more afraid of a posse—but it takes time to get them things organized. They can't do it in a hour or two. Besides, if they raise a posse, it'll have to be in another town because I got a gun on the operator where I am. No message is going through to the local law.''

Ed persisted. ''Why won't they grab us when we pick up the money?''

''Well, we tell 'em if they don't want the prince hurt, they stay away. We still got 'im, and he's our ace in the hole. We tell 'em to put the money in a certain place and stay away from it. One of us picks up the money, *then* we tell 'em where the prince is. Won't that work?''

Ed scratched his jaw. ''Don't that mean you have to wire 'em twice?''

Nate pursed his lips. Could it be done with one wire? He counted on his fingers. ''One, we tell 'em we got the prince. Two, we want a hunnerd thousand for him. Three, we tell 'em where to drop the money—and to stay away. Four, we pick up the money and git out. Five, we wire 'em where the prince is.''

Ed nodded. ''That's better. What place you got in mind for them to put the money?''

''I dunno—we got to think about that.''

Will spoke for the first time. ''What if they don't believe you?''

''What?'' They both stared at him.

''What if they don't believe we got the prince?''

Nate growled. ''Hell, we send 'em something that belongs to him.''

''And that'll take another month. . . .''

''Besides,'' Nate said. ''The prince is missin', ain't he? We got him. When we tell them we got him, they're going to believe us. How'd we know he was missin', else?''

''That's right,'' Ed said admiringly. ''But we ought to send 'em something just the same. I seen him wearin' a nice silver watch. How about that? Maybe it got his name in it.''

''Good idea. I could leave it with the telegraph operator to give to them when they show up.''

Ed got out the makin's and began to roll a cigarette. ''I guess that's it. When you want to do it?''

Chapter Eighteen

LAREDO and Pete moved out away from the stream, looking for tracks. It was possible the prince had tried to cross the stream and had been swept off his horse. But since they had not found his body the chances were, Laredo thought, he had managed to save himself.

Pete said, "Why would he want to cross the stream?"

Laredo shrugged. "I dunno why, but we found his horse in it. That's pretty good evidence that he might have been in it too. Maybe he lost direction in the storm."

"Umm, maybe. But he ought to know better than to cross a stream."

"Let's assume he didn't. Maybe he tried to—for some reason of his own, and didn't make it. So, if we assume he's still on this side—where is he?"

"All right, let's assume it. He'd want to find shelter first thing."

"Logical." Laredo nodded. "It's raining and it's cold. He'd want to get out of the storm—so we look around for a promising spot."

There were few likely places for shelter and they investigated all of them within the day's ride. Before dark they met Voss and the others near the stream. The water level was much lower, the stream had lost its anger, and Voss talked about crossing it in the morning to search the other side.

Voss was desperate. Knarig had very little food with him and was not a forager.

Charlie said to Laredo, "The prince's chances ain't good, not afoot. If we don't find 'im in the next couple of days . . ." He shook his head sadly. "He got no experience of this-here country, and if he met Indians they'd take 'is scalp like that!" He snapped his fingers. "A white man afoot!"

They continued the search at sunup, riding far apart, converging now and then to explore ravines or other formations that might provide shelter in a storm.

Near the end of the day they came upon a stand of trees in a low-lying section, and upon dismounting and walking through it, they found the remains of a campfire.

"It could be his," Laredo said.

Pete nodded, looking about. "But why didn't he stay here? He knew we'd look for him."

"If he had a compass with him, he might have started walking south."

Pete smiled. "I doubt if he did—have a compass. But it's a fool thing, walking across the prairie."

"He's a prince. Do we know how he thinks?"

Pete rolled a cigarette and struck a match. "It's a fool thing. If he'd stayed here we'd have him now."

"Let's look for tracks."

They came upon a well-marked trail at once. It led from the wood across the plain, straight as an arrow, south and east. Three horses.

Pete frowned at them. "Three horses. We could be on the wrong track."

"Unless someone else found him first."

"I suppose it's possible. . . ."

Laredo said, "This is a big, lonely country. How many people could be wandering around in the rain?"

"We've been searching a couple of days," Pete said reasonably. "This is the only trail we've come across. Why not follow it a way and see what develops."

"Like what?"

Pete nudged his horse. "Keep an open mind, amigo."

In the next mile they came upon a large, wet, sandy area. The tracks left a dark trail on the ground. Pete halted and slid down at once to look closely at the imprints.

Laredo joined him. "What is it?"

Pete touched the tracks delicately. "See here—this shoe has a deep nick in it. It shows clearly." He indicated other prints of the same shoe. "Do you see anything else that's different about it?"

Laredo studied the trail, walking along it, careful not to step on it. He looked at Pete. "It's a bigger, heavier horse than the others."

Pete grinned. "That's right. It could be a bigger horse, but what if it's carrying two men?"

"Ahhh, very good. I think you've hit it. Let's follow along and see if the weight changes horses."

Pete looked at the dark sky. "Tomorrow. We'd better go back to the trees for now."

They made a fire in the same place in the wood and spent the night. Laredo wrote out a short note to Voss, saying they were following what they believed to be the track of men who had the prince. He put it in a pile of stones where he was sure it would be seen.

As they started out in the morning Pete said, "It has to be the prince. Nothing else makes much sense."

"Remember that underground character—Karl something . . . Jung. Maybe he found Knarig."

"Why would he take him anywhere? We were told he'd shoot the prince on sight."

Laredo nodded. The situation was getting complicated.

John Fleming was asked for regular reports. He had to admit he'd heard nothing from his two Tanner operatives. He was certain they had not received his message to recall the prince or they would have replied at once.

"They're still out in the wilds," he said. "There's nothing we can do but wait."

His superiors fumed, but Fleming was right, of course.

Nate Tinkler made the long ride south to the railroad, composing the message in his mind as he went, changing it and editing it a hundred times. It took eight days to reach the shining rails and most of another day to ride eastward, following the tracks to the little burg of Mecklin, a shop town made up of railroad employees.

There were sidings and shops with forges and repair facilities and barrack-like buildings where men lived. The town itself was tiny, only a few stores and saloons—and a telegraph office.

Nate entered the office in the morning. He took a half hour to print out his message, addressing it to the President of the United States in Washington City. He had no idea who else to send it to. Theirs was an important demand, after all. The president should be interested.

The telegrapher was a middle-aged man with white whiskers and spectacles perched on a beak nose. He read the long message with mounting alarm, glancing up at Nate several times as he perused it.

"You kidnapped the prince?"

Nate drew his Colt and laid it on the counter. The other stared at it. "No need f'that, sir."

"Send the message. I don't want no sermon."

The telegrapher nodded and sat down at his key. "You can't send a message direct to the president, mister."

"Send it like I wrote it—to his office."

The other shrugged and began tapping it out.

Nate walked around the little office. It was a small, square room with glass on three sides. He could see most of the one-street town and part of the railroad shops off to the right. There was no activity in the street at all. A few wagons were parked near the stores, with half a dozen horses waiting here and there in hitch racks. A dog was asleep in the middle of the street.

After the message had been sent, the key chattered and the telegrapher muttered, glancing at Nate, "They don't believe it."

Nate fished in his pocket and brought out the prince's silver watch. He pushed it across the counter. "Tell 'em you got this."

The older man examined the watch, reading the fancy engraving. He nodded and sat at the key again. In a few minutes he looked around. "They're authenticating the watch."

"What's that mean?"

"They have to make sure it *is* the prince's watch."

Nate scowled. "How long's that going to take?"

The telegrapher shrugged lightly. "I can't tell you. I just work for the railroad."

Nate took a turn about the office, staring through the windows. How long could he afford to wait here? He asked, "How far's the next town?"

"About sixty miles."

"On the railroad?"

"Yes."

Nate grunted, wondering if the old man was telling the truth. He'd been in the office an hour now. As soon as they got the message they would probably set things in motion to catch him—no matter what he told them.

The key chattered and the telegrapher jotted on a slip of paper. "They want to know about the prince. Is he alive?"

"Of course he's alive! Soon's they give us the money we'll tell where he is."

The key tapped that out, and chattered again. "They want to know who you are."

"I'm the man who's got the prince! You tell 'em that. And you tell 'em I ain't answering no more questions."

"They want to know how many of you there are."

"Three. No more questions, dammit!"

Nate walked back and forth restlessly. He hadn't anticipated all this. In his mind it had been a cut-and-dried thing. The prince in exchange for the money. Simple. Like buying a side of beef. But those fools in Washington made everything complicated.

How long did he dare stay here?

Some sheriff might be getting a posse together in the next town, but that was hours away. The next train would surely bring government agents looking for him. He went outside and peered along the rails in both directions. Nothing was in sight.

But he knew he couldn't hang around much longer.

He went back into the office. "They going to send the money?"

The telegrapher shook his head. "I dunno. They had to

transmit your message to the right people. Then they had to authenticate the watch. I suppose now they're making up their minds what to do."

"I told 'em what to do!" They were stalling for time. He was sure of it. He pointed to the key. "You tell 'em if they want the prince back they got to do like I say."

"What d'you want me to tell them?"

"I already told them when I first come in here." Nate turned and went out to his horse. Let them stew in it for a while. He'd send another message later. He mounted the horse and headed west. Next time it would be different. The money or else!

Nate's message raised a furor in Washington. Prince Knarig had been kidnapped! Some country hick had sent a message to the president asking for money in exchange for the prince!

If officials had wanted to keep the situation quiet they were disappointed from the first. It was a secret that could not be kept. Newspeople sniffed it out and all the eastern newspapers spread it across the land, truth mixed with fantasy and drowned in sensation. The news was telegraphed everywhere and cabled to Europe and the world.

Nate Tinkler was astonished when he rode into Bonnet days later and saw the extras: PRINCE KIDNAPPED! Editors speculated wildly about where His Highness could be—they speculated about everything imaginable. They dug up everything possible about little Reichenbach—which most had never heard of. It filled columns.

There was actually little to tell, concerning the kidnapping. No one knew anything much. The kidnappers had demanded one hundred thousand dollars . . . and that was about it. A message had been sent by an unknown man from a little telegraph office in the middle of nowhere. The man in question had left an engraved silver watch with the telegrapher, which has been authenticated as belonging to the prince. The kidnapping was real enough.

John Fleming was called to another meeting with the Secretary of State, Mr. Peabody, who had been in constant communication with the Reichenbach foreign minister. Peabody, ordinarily the most polite of men, was visibly annoyed at the publicity. He had ordered an investigation in order to turn up those who had leaked information to the press.

"I know you had nothing to do with it, John."

Fleming made a gesture. "I'm afraid the publicity will hamper us a good bit, sir. Our chief worry is that the kidnappers will feel so threatened they will do away with the prince and hide his body."

"Let us pray that will not happen."

"Yes, sir."

"You've not heard anything from your men?"

"Not yet, sir. I have to assume they're still out of touch."

"The man who sent the message has disappeared?"

"Yes, but we have an excellent description of him from the telegraph operator. I've had men going through the files looking for likely characters from that area—men with records, you know. Two names jump out. Nate Tinkler and Iver Givens. I think Tinkler is our man. His name has turned up before."

"Ahhh, that's good. . . ."

"Yes, and there is a rumor that Givens was killed in a brawl in Texas. We're checking. But Tinkler fits the telegrapher's description."

"Stay with it then. Check into his friends. . . ."

"I will, sir. I hope to have a further report for you very soon."

"Excellent, John."

The cables from Reichenbach were stiffly formal, the phrases icily civil. But it was apparent to one accustomed to reading between lines that the foreign minister was very upset that the Americans had apparently been able to do nothing at all about locating Prince Knarig.

In Reichenbach the situation was tense. Prince Lothar was failing and his young son, Knarig, couldn't be found! The American government was ordered to agree to any price. It would be reimbursed.

Mr. Peabody replied to the cables, his language couched

in diplomatic tones. The American government was prepared to pay whatever ransom asked—as soon as communications could be restored with the unknown kidnappers, who had broken them off. Unfortunately everything had to wait until then.

Mr. Peabody assured the minister that his government hesitated to move against the kidnappers in any way for fear of endangering the prince's life.

Karl and Franz were astounded to read in the newspapers that the prince had been kidnapped! The fellow, Nate, had apparently somehow carried through his plan. How had he known where Knarig was?

The newspapers, lacking hard news, were having a frantic time printing anything at all pertaining to the Principality of Reichenbach. The ancient quarrel between the principality and the province that had gained its freedom a century ago was unearthed and discussed in the columns.

The cartoonists had a field day with the Movement, depicting bearded men slinking about with lighted fuses on black bombs. . . .

The kidnapping was a shock to Karl Jung. What could he say to his superiors? That he and Franz had done their best was not good enough. So he stayed away from the telegraph office, not wishing to receive bad news. The bad news was certain to be that he was doing too little. Of course, they were also certain to say he should have prevented the kidnapping. But how could he have?

The leaders of the Movement were far away across the ocean and obviously had no conception of the American West and its distances. A man might ride across Reichenbach in a day. But in America, a day's ride was not as much as a drop in the bucket.

The leaders of the Movement were sometimes very foolish. If they threatened him—he might just turn his back and stay in America!

Chapter Nineteen

THE trail they followed led straight to Bonnet. But within a few miles of the town it joined the road to Wendover and got lost in hundreds of other tracks.

Had the pursued gone into town or passed through or around it? There was no way to tell.

Pete said, "They're still here. They came straight to Bonnet. They could easily have given it a wide berth, but they didn't."

"Pretty good logic," Laredo agreed. "Are you a college graduate?"

"Yes, I am," Pete said gravely.

A side street had several boardinghouse signs. They selected one and paid the landlady for rooms and board. "I serve breakfast and supper. Dollar a day. I don't do no clothes washin'."

They paid her and went out to make the rounds of saloons, watching and listening, but heard no whisper concerning their quarry. If the three horses had come into Bonnet they had disappeared, it seemed, into thin air.

The telegraph line was also down, a not uncommon occurrence. Pilgrims used the insulators for targets and roving Indians were fond of pulling down the talking wire for the copper.

The telegrapher said, "You all can wait for the line to be repaired."

"How long will that take?"

"Could be tomorra or ten days. But you can always go south to the railroad."

They decided to wait—and keep looking.

Colonel Voss and the others arrived in Bonnet in a week. They had detoured to Wendover for victuals, and a day after they got to Bonnet the newspapers came out with the kidnapping story. It was the only subject talked about in the town, and Voss was raging and resigned by turns.

Laredo and Pete composed a wire to John Fleming, relating what they knew, and when the wire was repaired sent it off.

Nate and the Vinton brothers were astounded by the newspaper stories of the kidnapping. They had never imagined the act would cause so much commotion.

"You'd think we shot the goddamn president!" Ed said.

In every account Nate read the government reiterated that they were marking time, waiting for word from the kidnappers. Nothing could be done until communications were restored.

Ed said, "They want us to wire 'em, but won't they have every telegraph office surrounded? If you go into one, they's like to grab you. Then they'll squeeze it outa you where we are with His Honor."

"They can't surround every one. They don't have that many men."

"They could use the army."

"Wait a minute," Nate said. "I remember seein' a telegraph key at a water stop on the railroad, miles from any town. It's just the place."

"Maybe they'll figger you don't know about it," Ed said.

"That's right." Nate rolled his blankets and filled his possibles bag. He set out that afternoon, pointing south.

The third day out Nate was jumped by Indians as he stopped at a creek for water. The war party was a small band of young men who were looking for trouble. One white man alone was a prize! Nate got to the horse and headed for flat land as fast as the mount could carry him.

But the Indians ran him down in a matter of hours, shot the horse, then chased him on foot for several miles, yelling and hooting before they closed in. . . .

John Fleming's coded wire to Laredo stated the government's position in the matter of Prince Knarig. A second communication from the kidnappers was being awaited. Nothing would be done to collect the kidnappers until another ransom message was received, for fear of harm to the prince.

But thousands of flyers had been printed with Nate Tinkler's photograph from prison and a large reward for information leading to his arrest. These were being distributed in confidence to lawmen. The instant the money was paid and the prince released, the flyers would go to every person west of the Mississippi.

In Fleming's opinion, Tinkler would have to dig a hole somewhere and crawl in for the rest of his life to avoid capture.

Fleming cited the telegrapher's description of Tinkler. "He is undoubtedly our man."

"There's two others with him," Laredo said to Pete. "If you had to keep a man prisoner in secret, where would you go?"

"Any one of a thousand places. But if you want to keep him alive, you've got to feed him, so you'd stay close to a source of food."

"Like a town."

"Yes. Like Bonnet. It's ideal I'd think. It's big enough so men come and go constantly without drawing attention."

"You're guessing they might hold him outside of town?"

Pete shrugged elaborately. "Yes—if I'm guessing. I'd think it was less likely they'd have a place in town that's private and secure enough to hold a prisoner, without neighbors getting curious."

Laredo nodded. "I think you're exactly right. Especially about neighbors. I doubt if one of the kidnappers owns a house here."

"Not likely."

"Then we ought to snoop around."

* * *

The Vinton brothers quickly fell into a routine—of doing nothing. They settled down to wait for Nate's return. There was no work about the place to be done; in fact the less work the better. They did not want a wandering pilgrim to notice repairs or evidence of occupancy. When they chopped wood for the fire they did it inside the barn, and neither of them went outside without first making sure no one was about.

They kept fires to a minimum and only lighted one late at night when the smoke could not be seen. They kept the prince in a stall, his legs tied. Once a day they allowed him up, to walk about the barn for exercise, with one of the brothers sitting high up with a revolver handy.

Knarig no longer talked with either man. He accepted his role stolidly, refusing to answer questions, turning his back when they spoke to him. At first this treatment infuriated Ed and he withheld food from the prince. But Knarig never complained, and Ed gave it up.

They kept their two animals in adjoining stalls of the barn, out of sight. In fact, they lived in the barn. There was a room where a hired hand had slept in better times which they swamped out.

It drizzled and rained off and on and the time plodded by, much more slowly than they were used to. They slept a good deal, as did the prince, taking turns. Nate would probably be gone at least two weeks. Every day Ed made a slash mark on the wall to keep score.

There were eight slash marks on the wall the day that Ed noticed the two riders.

The two men walked their horses past the house in a light rain. They were several hundred yards distant. When they halted, Ed thought they were examining the place with binoculars.

He watched them through a crack in the barn wall. Both Will and the prince were napping. The strangers took their time, but they did not come closer. Finally they went on and disappeared, walking the horses.

When Will woke, Ed mentioned the riders.

"They didn't come in here, did they?" Will made a face.

"No, but they looked at the house."

Will said, "What you gettin' at, Ed?"

"Maybe we ought to git out of here."

Will was astonished. "We got to wait for Nate! How's he going to find us if we ain't here?"

"Lissen—if they catch us with *him*, then we're finished! We'll never get out of jail. They'll throw the key away and forget about us."

Will sighed deeply. "I think you're chewin' the bit. Anyway, we ain't got another horse. It's a pain in the ass ridin' double."

"I'll go get one tomorra."

His brother shook his head. "If we leave here, how's Nate going to find us?"

"We'll hafta find him."

Will grumbled. Ed had always been the leader, but finding Nate might be impossible, especially out on the grass. They could miss him even if he were within shouting distance. Besides, it would take all three of them to pull off the kidnapping. Ed was probably just getting itchy and restless, doing nothing for too long. Leaving the barn, Will felt, might lose them everything.

But he had never been able to stand up to Ed.

Stealing a horse proved to be easy. Not so a saddle. Ed rode to the edge of town in a heavy cold rain in the dark. There were corrals everywhere, big and small ones. He had brought a rope hackamore with him. He looked over half a dozen horses in two corrals. When he decided on an animal, he got down and opened the gate, slipped the hackamore over the head of a gray, and led the horse out to the road. Then he quietly closed the gate again and went back to the barn, secure in the knowledge that his tracks would be blotted out by the rain.

His Honor would have to ride bareback, but that was better than walking.

When he returned, Will argued about going, but Ed would not change his mind. Seeing the two men so close had made him jumpy. They could be Pinkertons, arranging a raid on the old house this very minute.

They gathered their things together and left the house before dawn. Ed led them south toward the far-off railroad. It was still raining. With any luck they would meet Nate coming back.

Laredo and Pete started snooping, beginning with the houses, shacks, and tents closest to the town. There were dozens of them and many took only a glance. It was apparent that three men and horses could not fit into most of the shacks and lean-tos.

They quickly evolved a system: after ascertaining who lived in one house, they would ask the next likely one. They were looking for a brother who had come to Bonnet, Laredo told the householders. He was somewhere in town, probably staying with two friends.

People were eager to help, but no one knew of three men living in the same house together.

They moved farther and farther out from the town, investigating every sort of shelter including caves, but without result.

Then, in the rain, about four miles from town, they came on a weatherbeaten, run-down, deserted house and barn in a ragged clump of trees. They halted and peered at it.

Pete said, "It's exactly the sort of hideaway they might pick."

Laredo used the binoculars. "I don't see any sign of life . . . no chickens or stock . . . no smoke . . ." He passed the glasses over.

Pete said, "Let's go on by as if we're not interested. If the people we're after are in there let's not spook them."

"Yes. They'll probably have a fire tonight. It's turning cold." He nudged the horse and they moved on.

In town they reported to Voss what they had seen and suspected. Laredo suggested they enlist the local law and surround the old house at once.

Voss shook his head. "We will enlist the law, but we will

go in just after dawn. It's the time when they will be least on their guard."

The law was a deputy sheriff named Billings. He agreed with Voss, deputized two other men, and they all rode out to the vicinity of the old house in the rainy dark. Thunder rumbled above them and the icy rain forced them to bundle up. At dawn they had the place surrounded and moved in slowly . . . to find the house and barn deserted.

In the mealy light it was apparent that several horses had left the barn and headed south, but the rain was methodically eliminating the tracks. They could not tell how many horses had passed.

They had no provisions with them so it was necessary to return to Bonnet to get them.

It had been a frustrating experience, but Voss had the grace to say he'd been wrong. They should have hit the house and barn as Laredo had suggested.

Chapter Twenty

ED and Will Vinton had been selected by Nate Tinkler to help in the kidnapping because they were hardcases. Not because they were brainy. Ed, he thought, was possibly smart enough not to crawl into the barrel of a loaded cannon, but no one could be sure about Will.

But as they rode south from the old Ferguson place, even Ed began to have second thoughts. He had insisted they go, and now he worried they would not meet Nate. According to the original plan, Nate would return to the old house when he had wired the government and completed the arrangements satisfactorily.

If they did not meet Nate, how would they know what arrangements had been made?

They kept a sharp lookout, but it was a vast land; they could easily miss Nate. It nagged at Ed. Maybe they ought to go back.

When he discussed his fears with Will the other said, "But I thought the law might find us there!"

"By now they prob'ly been there and gone—if they was going to go there in the first place. If we don't meet Nate, what the hell we gonna do?"

Will glanced at the prince, who was sitting on his horse, staring at them. "Maybe we could sell 'im to somebody."

Ed frowned at his brother. Sell the prince? He had never thought of it in those terms, but that was what they were doing, trying to sell the prince to the government.

He said, "We got to find Nate. He prob'ly got it all laid out nice and smooth by now. We better take a chance and go back to the old house. That's the only place he knows to find us."

Will had to agree it was true. He turned around reluctantly.

They went back by a different route, and as they started it began to snow lightly.

The first night, as they made camp, Charlie Bennett had a talk with Voss. "You don't need me no longer. With the prince gone, you're not goin' to be hunting anymore this year."

Voss nodded. "You want to be paid off?"

"Yes. I got personal matters t'take care of. That all right with you?"

Voss did not argue. He counted out the agreed-upon money and Charlie shook hands all around, mounted his horse, and headed east, after giving Voss an address in St. Louis where he could be reached.

In the morning they continued riding south till they reached the railroad tracks—with nothing in sight in either direction. There's nothing so lonely, Laredo thought, as bare steel rails on the treeless plains.

Pete flipped a coin and they pointed west.

The next day an eastbound freight passed them, and two days later they came into Triton. It was a tired and weathered little whistle-stop in cattle country.

The telegraph office was open and a skinny man in a green cardboard eyeshade looked at Laredo's credentials.

"What d'you want to know, mister?"

"Did someone send a wire from here recently concerning a kidnapping?"

"You mean that one's been in all the papers? No, sir."

A key was clicking as they spoke. "You hear all the messages up and down the line?"

The operator nodded. "Nobody sent anything about a kidnapping—not since that first one."

It was disappointing. Laredo went out to the others.

Voss said, "It means they went somewhere else—or haven't sent it yet."

"Damn strange if they haven't sent it," Laredo said. "They want the money. Why would they hold back?"

No one had an answer.

He and Pete encoded a message to John Fleming, telling him where they were, asking if the kidnappers had contacted Washington.

Fleming's return wire said they had not. His superiors were still waiting for some word so the ransom could be paid. Fleming speculated that the kidnappers, being new at the game, had panicked on reading the lurid newspaper stories. "Maybe they are afraid to enter a telegraph office."

It's as good an explanation as any, Laredo thought.

"There's nothing to do but wait," Pete said, a thing that Voss hated to hear.

Voss and the Reichenbach foreign minister had been in communication in Bonnet, and now he sent a wire from Triton and learned by return message that Prince Lothar was in a coma and sinking. The doctors did not give him long. If Prince Knarig died—a terrible thought—his sister, Nadya, would come into power. But as long as the issue was in doubt the government would be leaderless. A bad situation. Voss was pressed to do all he could.

They stayed overnight at the only hotel and discussed their options. The kidnappers wanted money, but to get it they had to wire Washington. Why hadn't they done it?

Laredo said, "There are more telegraph facilities along the railroad than anywhere else. It's their best opportunity."

Ed and Will Vinton returned to the old house and barn without meeting anyone. It snowed part of the way but let up, and the sun came out the last two days.

Nate was not in the house or barn and there was no evidence that he'd been there.

"He ain't back yet," Ed said. "He woulda left something to show."

They had almost no provisions left. Early in the morning Ed rode into town and brought back two gunny sacks of food.

He had listened in a saloon, he said, and the talk was that the kidnappers of the prince had not replied to Washington as promised. The entire thing was hanging fire.

Will said in astonishment, "But that's what Nate went to do!"

Ed was equally disturbed. "Well, they said he never done it."

"You figger something happened to Nate?"

"It's been a couple weeks now. He sure as hell should have sent that message." Ed frowned at his brother. "I wonder if the damn gover'ment is tellin' the truth."

"You mean they don't want to pay us?"

"Maybe," Ed said darkly. "How you figger them politicians? You r'member that sheriff down in West Texas? The one who broke us out for forty dollars? Hell, you can't trust politicians."

"Maybe Nate got scared off and had to go to another telegraph—that could take time."

Ed nodded, sighing. "Yeah. Let's open a can of beans. His Honor must be hungry."

"I think they're holed up somewhere," Pete said. "Traveling with the prince would be difficult for any length of time."

Voss studied him. "Go on."

"Well, for one thing, they can't take a prisoner into a town. It would be too obvious. If they move about, someone is apt to see them, even out on the grass."

"That's right," Laredo agreed. "And the reward is substantial."

Voss growled. "But why haven't they wired Washington?"

Laredo shrugged. "They probably don't trust what they hear."

"But sooner or later they're going to have to!"

"Let's hope they don't panic."

Waiting was hard on the nerves. They decided to go out looking again. They had not investigated all the possibilities around Bonnet. The weather was holding, cold but not snowing. Winter was just around the corner.

It had to be methodical work, snooping into every isolated shack. It was necessary to treat each one as if the kidnappers were inside with cocked weapons, ready to shoot them on sight. It made for slow going. Days went by and they made no progress.

The Vinton brothers were increasingly restless. They were unused to being cooped up like housecats. Nate had not appeared, and Ed was voicing his opinion every few hours that either something had happened to him or he had decided to skedaddle and leave them holding the bag.

"Damn him, I bet you he just went on south, maybe even on down into Mexico."

"Why would he do that?"

"Too goddamn much risk. If they catch us, little brother, they going to stick us in a well one hunnerd feet deep."

Will said, "Maybe the law got him and he's in jail right now. That's why he can't come back."

"Maybe . . ."

"What you figger? Are we gonna wait till he gits out?"

Ed scowled. "No, we can't. We ain't got a dollar between us. His Honor is cleaned out, too. We got to git money to live on."

"Why don't *we* send that wire?"

Ed looked at Will, considering. "I guess we could."

"It'd be better'n staying here doing nothing, wouldn't it?"

"Yeah, that's right."

They rolled their blankets again, got the prince on the horse bareback, and set out, moving toward the distant railroad.

They followed much the same track as before and made good progress under a weak sun that warmed them not at all. They saw no one and went all the way to the twin rails—and had a bit of luck. Far off to the east was a column of smoke rising into the still air.

They rode toward it cautiously. It came from the chimney

of a house where there was a lonely water tower, a corral, some sheds, and nothing else.

"The train stops there for water," Ed said. "Maybe they got a telegraph key, too."

They watched the house for an hour but saw only two men. One was older and walked with a stoop, the other was hammering at a shed near the small house. Apparently they were the only souls present. There were two horses in the corral.

Ed said, "You stay here with His Honor. I'll go in and see if they got a telegraph."

There were some trees and a line of low sheds paralleling the tracks, and at the end of the sheds was a small shack. As Ed rode in the stooped man came to the door of the shack. "Howdy."

Ed smiled, seeing the key inside the shack. "You the telegraph man?"

The other nodded. He wore a trainman's cap and had a deeply lined face. "Don't send no private messages though. You got to go to Triton for that. About thirty-five mile." He pointed west.

Ed stepped down, drew his revolver, and pushed the man inside with the muzzle. "I hope you going to change your mind, friend."

It was a tiny room, barely enough space for two, a chair and a bench. The second man continued pounding with a hammer.

The telegrapher said with a sigh, "What you want to send?"

"I got a message to go to Washington City."

"Who to?"

"I dunno a name." Nate had never mentioned a name.

He frowned at the older man who suddenly pointed a finger. "You're one of the kidnappers!"

Ed pushed the other into the chair. "You tell Washington we got the prince and we want a hunnerd thousand for him."

"Tell Washington? You got to have a name. Who do I send it to?"

"How the hell do I know? Tell 'em it's important." Ed poked the other with the revolver. "Send it."

The older man made a hopeless gesture and turned to the key, tapping out the message rapidly. He was sure his visitor could not read the code so he included his name and the station, asking for help. The message, he knew, would cause a sensation—and it did. It took a while to get through to Washington, but important people were expecting it.

When the return came he jotted it down and handed the paper to Ed, who said, "Read it."

"It asks for instructions. What do you want done with the money?"

Ed had thought about that particular. "Tell 'em to put it in a bag and toss if off the train twenty miles east of Triton—and do it tomorrow."

The operator nodded and the key chattered and clicked. Then he turned. "They want to know where the prince is. Is he all right?"

"He's fine. Soon's I git the money I'll tell 'em where to find 'im."

The key clicked again. The older man sent the message, adding that he had not seen the prince or any other person and suggested this one might be a fake. He said to Ed, "They want to know who you are."

Ed shook his head. "They got the message. That's all."

He had seen an axe outside by one of the sheds. He holstered the pistol and stepped outside and brought it in. As the other yelled, he smashed the key and chopped the wires.

Then he mounted the horse and rode away.

Chapter Twenty-one

"THE man might be a fake," John Fleming said, reading the wire, "an opportunist, but we can't take a chance, as I see it. He might not be."

Secretary Peabody's forehead furrowed. "One hundred thousand dollars is a lot of money to throw out of a train window. Are there any precautions we can take?"

"They want the money immediately, and there's no way to negotiate. The kidnapper has gone back wherever he came from." Fleming stepped to a huge wall map. "But he has to be in this area." He circled it with a finger.

"How fast can we get troops there?"

"Not fast enough, sir. He's given us no time at all."

"What about your Tanner agents?"

"I've been trying to reach them, Mr. Secretary, but they're out searching."

Peabody slumped in his chair. "Damn. Then I'm afraid you're right. We have to take the chance." He smiled bleakly. "Of course, it's Reichenbach's money."

Ed and Will Vinton were jubilant. The government would have a hundred thousand dollars tossed out of a train window for them, the next day, near Triton.

Neither of them slept that night. They talked endlessly about what they were going to do with the money. The next day they were both bleary-eyed and tired. They rode to a spot opposite the tracks, but a mile distant from them, and waited.

Finally an engine and coal car arrived, chugging along the track, trailing black smoke. They had demanded the money the next day, which was not a scheduled run, so an engine had to be pressed into service. Ed and Will watched it go by and disappear into the distance. They galloped the horses to the tracks at once. The money had to be in a satchel of some kind, and had to be near the tracks—how far could a man throw it?

It was not where they expected it would be.

Will asked, "How far is twenty miles from Triton, Ed?" He peered along the shining rails. "Maybe we in the wrong place."

"Keep lookin'," Ed growled. "It could be on either side of the goddam tracks."

They did not find it that day.

Ed was apprehensive. Maybe the government had decided not to give them the money! But they had the prince. Of course, the satchel could be anywhere along a ten mile stretch of roadbed. The government wouldn't make it easy, damn them. If the satchel was the color of the brush that lined the tracks, it might take a week to find it.

Ed growled to himself. He should have insisted on them tossing out a red tablecloth with the money. It hadn't occurred to him it would be this difficult.

They didn't find it the next day either.

They camped by the tracks each night. They did not find the satchel after five days of searching. Both Ed and Will were positive they had been tricked. There was no money.

In Washington, after five days of waiting, the tension was thick. No word had been received concerning the prince. It was feared the kidnappers had the money and had probably killed and buried Knarig.

Laredo, Pete, and the others reached Triton, where they wired Fleming and learned the money had been delivered as required. But the prince had not been released.

That very day, Fleming told them, the thousands of posters

bearing the reward information and the picture of Nate Tinkler would be put up across the nation.

Fleming also directed them to go at once to the area where the money had been dropped off. "See what you can learn. It's our last connection with the kidnappers."

They went immediately, leaving Voss and Emil behind. Voss had become increasingly difficult and they were glad to get away by themselves.

The kidnapper's instructions had been vague: "Drop off the money twenty miles east of Triton."

How did one measure twenty miles? Laredo said, "It could be roughly calculated by the engine's speed. . . ."

"But the drop area could be miles long. How far would they fling the bag?"

"And on which side of the tracks?"

Prince Knarig was in the prime of his life, young and vigorous. He had been in the military in Reichenbach and had gone through rigorous training—as all royal sons did. He was in excellent health. His leg had healed, though he had a very slight limp.

If he had not been young and strong he might not have survived Ed and Will Vinton's treatment. They pushed and shoved him with no regard for anything. They barely fed him, gave him one thin blanket, and made him ride bareback for days. They tied his hands and feet each night so he slept poorly, and the young one, Will, harassed him constantly with his pistol barrel. Knarig was bruised from shoulders to hips.

But he gave them little to complain about. He kept his eyes open as they traveled and he did his best not to make them suspicious. He was passive and silent, biding time.

Then one night, after his captors had been searching for the bag with the money for a week, the prince was able to work loose the rope that bound his wrists. Silently he untied his feet.

Ed was asleep a few yards away but Will was sitting up, on guard. They took turns. However, Will's eyes were closed and he seemed to be asleep, breathing regularly.

Knarig itched to get close enough to grab the revolver he knew Ed carried. But he could not see the weapon in the dark. Maybe Ed was lying on it.

Knarig moved cautiously. He was completely dressed, even to boots, and peeled the blanket off, turning onto hands and knees, his eyes on Will. With infinite caution he moved away from the camp. The three horses were picketed a dozen feet away, and he thought about trying for one but decided against it. It could not be done silently, and he had great respect for the brothers' ability with pistols.

He slipped away into the brush, moving in as straight a line as possible to put as much distance between them as he could before they discovered he was gone. He knew where the railroad tracks were, and that Triton was off to the west. He would try to get to the town, miles away.

It was a dark night with overcast clouds and it made for slow going. A mile or more from the camp he headed for the rails and ran along beside them in the open. It was better than pushing through brush.

Every moment or two he looked back, expecting to see one of them galloping after him.

After an hour he began tiring. They had given him almost nothing to eat the day before. Their provisions were about gone; they had talked about one of them going into town for more . . . or about hunting game. Neither had expected to be searching for the money for a week.

Then he heard the horse. Instantly he ducked away from the rails into the thick brush and lay motionless. In a minute Ed came galloping the horse beside the rails. He went past and Knarig got up, hearing the hoofbeats fade away.

Will had more than likely gone in the other direction looking for him. They were probably in a rage!

Knarig looked at the lowering sky. How long until dawn? He had no idea. But he'd be wise to find a place to hide himself. They were capable of shooting him out of hand, especially the young one, Will.

The rails east of Triton ran straight across the plain, unswerving, shimmering dully in the light. Far off to the south it was probably raining. The clouds seemed to hug the earth in a gray veil.

Laredo and Pete walked their horses, one on either side of the roadbed, heading out of town. Earlier they had talked to the engineer who had made the special run from Triton to the next whistle-stop and who had tossed out the bag they had given him. It had been a gray-green, heavy canvas satchel with a padlock on it. He had slung it out into the weeds, guessing a bit about the distance from town.

"All that country looks the same," he'd said. "It's somewhere there, along the tracks."

They saw the distant rider near evening of the first day. The man was halted on the tracks and when he noticed them, he fired at them four times with a rifle.

Pete said, "He's trying to scare us away."

"Try a shot," Laredo said. Pete was better than most with a rifle.

Levering the Winchester, Pete looked at the sky, stood in the stirrups, and brought the muzzle down slowly. When he fired the far-off horse skittered. Then the rider turned and galloped off.

"That was close," Laredo said.

"I think I hit him."

They followed the horseman and in less than a mile saw the horse stumble and go down, thrashing for a moment before it lay still.

The rider quickly ducked behind the carcass, poked his rifle over the belly and fired at them.

Halting, they spread out widely and Pete fired back several times, forcing the man's head down. They quickly got into positions that allowed the man no cover, and when the fire got too hot he raised his hands and stood up.

They moved in slowly, but the other had given up. He had been hit just below the knee, a crease that was probably very painful. At Laredo's order, he tossed his pistol away.

"Who're you? Deputies?"

"Government agents," Laredo said, stretching the truth a mite. "Which of the kidnappers are you?"

The man sighed deeply. "Name's Ed Vinton."

"Where's the prince?"

Ed shook his shaggy head. "Don't know. He got away from us yestiddy."

"Who is *us*?"

"M'brother is out there somewheres."

Pete asked, "What happened to Nate Tinkler?"

Ed shook his head again. "Dunno that either. He never showed up."

"What have you done with the money?"

"Ain't got the goddamn money! Never found it! They never sent it, damn 'em!"

"Yes, they did," Laredo assured him. "If you haven't found it, it's still out there in the brush somewhere." He smiled at the other's scowl.

Vinton led them back to the camp where the prince had escaped in the night. "He run out on foot."

"Where have you looked for him?"

"Up and down the tracks. We figgered he might hit for the town."

"Did he have any food with him?"

Ed shrugged. "We din't have much—not after a week."

They flagged down the next train and had the conductor lock Vinton in an empty room to be turned over to the law in the next town.

Then they went looking for the prince.

They rode along the tracks and fired a rifle at five- or six-minute intervals, hoping Knarig would think it a rescue party. And he did. He came stumbling out of a ravine, waving his arms. He looked half-dead.

They gave him water and what food they had. "I left the frying pan for the fire," he said. "I was beginning to think I would die in that gulley."

But with food in his stomach, the prince declared himself fit to travel. He got up behind Laredo and they pointed toward town.

Knarig's rescue was sensational news and every newspaper in the land spread the story over its pages. He and Colonel Voss went at once to New York to take ship for Europe.

But Will Vinton was still at large. The case could not be closed until he was brought in. Laredo and Pete slipped out of town during the celebration—not wanting to be interviewed by the press, in any event. The credit was given to "two government agents, names withheld."

Will Vinton found the satchel.

He made a slit under the padlock with his knife and peered at the tightly packed greenbacks inside, his heart racing.

He tied the bag on behind the cantle and went looking for Ed but did not find him. He rode almost to Triton till he gave up and headed back. Where the hell was he? First Nate disappeared, now Ed.

Well, he could think of only one thing to do. Nate would do the same—head back to Bolton. Then they would divvy the money.

Of course, he would spend a little of it first. . . .

Karl Jung and Franz read the newspapers in Bonnet. The prince had been rescued and was on a train to the east. All their efforts had been in vain . . . no matter how hard they had tried.

But the shocker was a wire that came for them from the Movement. He and Franz were ordered home to face a tribunal. They would be tried for their failure.

"And undoubtedly found guilty," Karl said.

Of course the tribunal in Reichenbach had no idea of the vastness of the American West, nor the immense difficulties . . .

Karl fingered the telegram form and looked at Franz. Then he slowly tore the form into shreds as Franz smiled.

The next day they bought tickets for San Francisco and boarded the stage west.

Chapter Twenty-two

"ME and Will lived in Bolton," Ed said, "and hung out at the Union Saloon."

It was enough.

Laredo and Pete Torres walked their horses into the drab little town near evening and got down in front of the saloon. It was a Wednesday and the street was quiet. Inside a piano player pounded out tunes in the rear of the long room, but only a half-dozen men were present.

They had a description of Will: short, dark, built like a stump, and not the brightest. He was not in the saloon.

A bartender said he hadn't seen Will that day, but one of the girls said he was upstairs with Cora.

The stairs were outside on the end of the building. They went up quickly and found themselves in a dark hall. There was a hanging lantern, turned low, at the far end. On either side of the hall were doors.

Pete said, "Which one is Cora's?"

The doors were numbered with white paint, but no names. As they looked at them one opened and a girl came out, tugging at her dress. She saw them and paused, with the door still open, patting her hair. "Hello there. . . ."

Laredo asked, "Are you Cora?"

The girl shook her head. "Cora! No, she's in Two—if she's there." She smiled and went past them quickly and down the stairs.

She had come from Number Nine. They looked at the

closed door of Number Two, and out of the corner of his eye, Laredo saw the door of Number Nine move.

He yelled, "Look out!" and dropped to the floor, pulling his colt. Will Vinton, in pants and long johns, without boots, came around the door, firing.

Laredo's three shots centered him, and he was flung back along the floor. His heels thumped, and the pistol clattered away.

Pete was in a crouch by the wall, his pistol extended, but he hadn't fired. He glanced at Laredo. "The girl lied to us, amigo."

"That's a problem with dance-hall girls. . . ." Laredo went to the downed man. Will was very dead.

In the room they found the gray-green satchel, still full of money.

About the Author

ARTHUR MOORE is the author of thirteen westerns including THE KID FROM RINCON, TRAIL OF THE GATLINGS, THE STEEL BOX, DEAD OR ALIVE, MURDER ROAD, and ACROSS THE RED RIVER, published by Fawcett Books. He lives in Westlake Village, California, where he is at work on a new Bluestar Western.